Van

June 24, 2019

WITHDRAWN

SHARPSHOOTER

SHARPS

HOOTER

A NOVEL
OF THE
CIVIL WAR

David Madden

THE UNIVERSITY OF TENNESSEE PRESS ❖ KNOXVILLE

In very different form, parts of this novel originally appeared in *The Southern Review, Gettysburg Review, The South Dakota Review, The Black Warrior Review, The New Orleans Review, Xavier Review, Appalachian Heritage,* Homewords anthology, *Louisianna English Journal, Cultural Vistas, New Letters, Gulf Coast Collection of Stories and Poems, The East Tennessee Historical Society's Publications,* and *The Bread Loaf Anthology of Contemporary American Short Stories.*

Frontis: photograph reprinted by permission of Lightfoot Collection.
Page 1: photograph reprinted by permission of Bill Collins.
Page 53: photograph reprinted by permission of Gordon Cotton, director Old Court House Museum.
Page 89: photograph courtesy of Library of Congress.
Page 141: photograph courtesy of Library of Congress.

The paper in this book meets the minimum requirements of the American National Standard for Permanence of Paper for Printed Library Materials. ∞ The binding materials have been chosen for strength and durability.

✿ Printed on recycled paper.

LIBRARY OF CONGRESS CATALOGING-IN-PUBLICATION DATA

Madden, David, 1933–
　　Sharpshooter : a novel of the Civil War / David Madden. — 1st ed.
　　　p.　cm.
　　ISBN 0-87049-948-3 (cloth: alk. paper)
　　1. United States—History—Civil War, 1861–1865—Fiction.
I. Title.
PS3563.A339S48　1996
813'.54—dc20
　　　　　　　　　　　　　　　　　　　　96-9994
　　　　　　　　　　　　　　　　　　　　CIP

IN MEMORY OF PEGGY BACH:

"I AM THE AZURE BELL."

Contents

SHARPSHOOTER

"My Story"

"Let the Bridges Be Burned!"

Now! I will commence writing this down on my twenty-eighth birthday, Tuesday, July 25, 1876, on the Mountain. This is all true. Except for the lies that come naturally when you tell your own story.

Come to think about it, I was born in a tower—the loft of a cabin, high on a Mountain.

My name is Willis Carr, born July 25, 1848, on the south side of Holston Mountain, Carter County, in East Tennessee, on Stony Creek, which empties into the Watauga River near the Virginia and North Carolina borders.

Who are my folks? My father was George Carr, born on the Mountain, drowned with fifteen hundred others on the *Sultana* on the Mississippi River at the end of the War.

My mother was Jessie Willis, born below in Elizabethton, still living.

Well, we were up on the Mountain, and I was thirteen years old. I was raised on this Mountain with my three older brothers (one hanged, the others killed) and three younger brothers and sisters, and my grandpa (who died in a Rebel prison), my grandma Carr (now dead), and my Great-grandfather Carr, dead but present, who crossed over from Ireland.

What was our religion? We were on Parson Brownlow's Holston Methodist Circuit decades before I was born.

What was our politics? We were all Unionists, except my mother, who came from a family of Rebel sympathizers down in Elizabethton.

And me . . . ? I heard them talk, but I didn't listen closely enough to have a mind of my own on the War.

My Greatgrandfather, the only one of us who could read, read aloud Parson Brownlow's *Whig,* the only Union paper in the South in those days, and it had to come to him all the way from Knoxville.

My grandpa told me that one night my Greatgrandfather came into the cabin from hunting, said, "I'm a-cold," went over there and stirred up the fire, sat down by it, and they say he never got up, and the fire never went out. My Greatgrandfather was sitting there, his back turned, when I was born, they say, and his thunderous voice is the first thing I remembered.

Even when the sun boiled on the doorsill, he never left the fire on the hearth. "For the Lord's sake, Grandpa," my mother would say, "you worry us all to death, sitting over there, staring at the fire all the time. Why don't you go sit in the doorway and let your bones get some sun?"

"Right here's my little piece of it—goes down at night, and I poke it up in the morning, all I need. Every day, just like that big bonfire in the sky, its heat warms me, I cook by its fire, and read by its light."

The *Whig* always arrived late dark. When Greatgrandfather heard his son, my grandpa, come into the clearing from Elizabethton, he would yell out the full name, *"Parson Brownlow's Knoxville Whig and Rebel Ventilator!"* and then he would yell out the motto on the masthead, "To the Union, the Constitution, and Law!" Worn out from the climb up the Mountain, his son would hand it to him, where he sat, waiting by the deadlooking ashes, that he would blow alive, starting fire, until he could read the fine print. I'd be up in the sleeping-loft, and when the rafters went to shaking, I knew he had got his paper, because he'd read that thing aloud. His voice woke me and everybody else, reading the *Whig* aloud, bringing the Parson into the cabin with us, his swelling spirit rising through the floor boards into the sleeping-loft.

When my grandma would ask, "Can't you read without that storm?" she always triggered an even louder burst of Brownlow buckshot against the walls and ceiling. No, he could not. He did not want solitary, private print, such as he got from the Bible. He wanted fire, explosion! from the chest out into the cabin, scalding phrases, smoking images. When he was done, he'd take a hammer and nail that paper to the wall, as if to declare, "Look yonder! That's it! Right there! What the man said!"

One night, Parson Brownlow exposed to the light of day the dark facts about an awful conspiracy. I felt the concussion, but what my Great-grandfather read aloud did not stay in my memory separate from the cataract of words I had heard from my birth to that night. That very copy is spread before me now, dated May 25, 1861.

"My Unionist friends and I are to be arrested after the election in June by a military force and taken in irons to Montgomery and either punished for treason or held as hostages to guarantee the quiet surrender of the Union men of East Tennessee.

"The facts of this conspiracy against the rights of American citizens, together with the names of those concerned in urging it on, all, will be left in the hands of reliable, bold and fearless men who will make them public at the proper time. The thousands of Union men of East Tennessee devoted to principle and to the rights and liberties of those who fall at the hands of these conspirators will be expected to avenge their wrongs.

"Let the railroad on which Union citizens of East Tennessee are conveyed to Montgomery in irons be eternally and hopelessly destroyed. Let the property of the men concerned be consumed and let their lives pay the forfeit, *and the names will be given!* Let the fires of patriotic vengeance be built upon the Union altars of the whole land and let them go out where these conspirators live like fires from the Lord.

"If we are incarcerated at Montgomery, or executed, all the consolation we want is to know that our partisan friends have visited upon our persecutors a most horrible vengeance. Let it be done, East Tennesseans, though the gates of hell be forced and the heavens be made to fall!"

Greatgrandfather summoned all us folks into the room and read it aloud again, and read it a third time, and my father, my grandpa, and my older brothers picked up from him and each other enough phrases to fill the cabin and to cover South Holston while we hunted, loud enough to burst the eardrums of bears and wildcats and to make littler critters roll over and kick off. They even took to hurling them like rocks at each other in mock anger, and in real anger, and at me, when I disobeyed or outshot them. I only remember the thunder of it, not actual phrases because to me then, and all during the war, words were like weather, and when you're *in* very good or very bad weather, especially out hunting, there is no yesterday or tomorrow. You don't remember.

Nor had I then any sense of time, of the connection between one time and another. I do know that one day a man who was a stranger to me, but not to my Greatgrandfather, climbed our Mountain, and my folks huddled around him while he spoke softly to them.

He wanted the Carrs to go off with him and some other men in a few days to burn a railroad bridge. A company of Confederate soldiers might be guarding the bridge, and they hoped they would find ol' Devil Davis's whole legion of fallen angels there. Because they meant to go and do it. Then I watched the stranger go back down the Mountain.

And because they always took me with them hunting or fishing or trapping, I just waited for the signal.

I was thirteen, taller than my father, and people mistook me for nineteen. I had seldom been down off the Mountain, and never even seen the north side. We hunted the south side, and hunting is all I ever did, wanted to do, hoped to do.

I was the best shot on the Mountain, but I was never allowed to say so. In my family, bragging was left to Davy Crockett in the tales folks told. My grandpa once said, "Don't brag on what you can do. Davy Crockett done took care of all *that*. *You* don't have to brag nothing, you just *do* it, and go 'bout your business." So nobody ever said, "You're the best," and I never said I was the best either, but I *knew* it.

My mother said she reckoned that when she got word we were all dead, she would go back down the Mountain, home to Elizabethton to her own people, who were Confederates, and take the little chaps with her. "Not that I can ever get away from Brownlow," she said, without even looking at Greatgrandfather Carr over by "the place of fire," as I called it when I was a child.

"Yes, they say I can be heard all the way to Richmond!"

"I don't think they'll do it," grandma said.

But came the day they got ready to go, and when grandpa gave the signal to get up and start off, I went right on with them—to burn the bridge, wherever that is, do something in the Civil War, whatever that is, do something for the Union, whatever that is, I didn't know, but I thought it was a good idea, it would be something *different.*

"What you doing, coming with us?" they said, turning around to look at me.

"What you think you're doing? You get on back up yan with the women, stay by your Greatgrandfather," my father told me. "And take care of them till we get back!"

That hurt me. Had they forgot I was the best shot in the family? And had they forgot I was the fastest, longest runner, too? Because when they took off on their horses, I kept right up with them around those Mountain paths—running. They trooped down the Mountain, and I followed, madder now than I was hurt. They tried to chase me off with scalding words and extravagant threats, but I kept a-coming. And my brothers pulled up and they reached down in the path and picked up rocks and started throwing at me like I was a mad dog.

Well, I *was* a mad dog by the time they got out of sight.

I caught up with them down on Stony Creek where two men were holding horses for the Carr clan. Except for one, the best of them at shooting.

They rode off laughing, maybe not at me, but laughing like when we went on a long hunt, except they sounded different, like it was some new animal they were tracking.

For a long ways, it wasn't hard to keep close behind, except for my blurry tears of rage, because going down was rough on the horses.

"You got a list of who all's supposed to go with us?"

"I don't need no list."

To me, it was just voices in the dark.

"Boys, we got many miles to go, and then when we're done, we got to get beyond their reach before daylight. When you're about to do something foolish, just remember John Brown, boys, and where *he* ended."

Others met up with us, coming from every direction. Thinking I belonged, one of them let me ride double.

I listened to the voices of strangers who had come together in the dark.

"It was fittin' to call John Brown's name tonight, but don't expect any more slaves to rally 'round *us* than around *him* at Harpers Ferry."

"They'll help their master slice you open just to get a extry 'tater."

"Slaves is so rare 'round here," said the man I rode double with, "I bet *this* boy ain't never even seed one." I got the feeling those close by in the dark thought he was talking about himself, not me, and I was glad to be hidden from my folks.

So many voices filled the dark, I stopped trying to guess who was speaking and concentrated on getting it clear what we were doing as we went along.

"What's you burnin', Ed?"

I did hear names called, but the only ones I knew were my own kin and, among the voices in the dark, even *they* were only voices.

"Parson Brownlow's editorial about the railroad bridges. Mem'rized it."

"Let's *hear* it."

"Bet he can't *recite* it."

"Bet he can—every word."

"Don't tax me. Said, 'Let the railroad on which Union citizens of East Tennessee are conveyed to Montgomery in irons be eternally and hopelessly destroyed! Let the property of the men concerned be consumed, and let their lives pay the forfeit—and the names will be given!'"

"'The names will be given!'"

"'Let the fires of patriotic vengeance be built upon the Union altars of the whole land—'"

"'The fires of patriotic vengeance—'"

"'The Union altars.'"

"Them that can read is blessed."

"He ain't reading, he's just remembering."

"—'and let'—you'uns hush—'and let them go out where these conspirators live, like the fires from the Lord.'"

"You're *looking* at the fires from the Lord."

"'If we are incarcerated at Montgomery—'"

"Who's that *we*?"

"Us Unionists!"

"Let somebody hand old *Brownlow* a torch, too, then!"

"There's them that *talks* good and them that *acts* good. Shut up."

"'Let our partisan friends visit upon our persecutors a most horrible vengeance! Let it be done, East Tennesseans, though the gates of hell be forced and the heavens be made to fall!'"

"'Force the gates of hell, men!'"

"'Let the heavens be made to fall!'"

"My daddy can remember when Brownlow come through here as a Methodist circuit rider and held camp meetings within earshot of hell." Clear as a bell, that voice was my grandpa's. "Scorched more souls than if you tossed a bucket of boiling water on an ant hill."

I no longer had to strain to know what they were saying.

"What's Captain Fry doing now?"

"Writing in that book again."

"Writing makes me itch."

"That's why I burnt Brownlow's editorial."

"You all planning to get captured?"

"Remember them that vowed to come, but stayed behind," said somebody I figured must be this Captain Fry whose name they kept calling. "Every man armed?"

I saw by the light of the moon the silhouette and shadows of their pistols and rifles.

"We may meet friend or foe on the roads. Pass by without a greeting."

The old Indian path widened into a road. On that fast-freezing mud the hooves were loud. The road later dwindled into a path.

"I just can't get used to seeing 'em."

"Yeah, trains don't look right, do they, cutting through this valley."

"Me, I'd sooner see a camel off the desert, or a elephant out of the jungle—more like they would belong."

"Makes me nervous, something movin' through here faster'n me on my horse can go."

"First time I saw one, looked like fun, but *now* look at the misery it's brought in here."

Trees and bushes were so tight about the narrow, curving roads, it was like we rode into caves and came out into the light and then rode into another one.

Fifty mouths were spitting tobacco juice into the windstream their swift horses made. "Jim, I'm getting that in the face every time. Spit it in your critter's ear."

In the dark, a bush stung my cheek, brushed my sleeve, another my leg.

"Stream crossing ahead!"

"Water under foot!"

"Thin out to ride this stream," yelled the voice I tagged Captain Fry's. "No use to drench each other."

We came to a ford where we crossed a river, then took another path no wider than a wagon bed.

A few miles further, I felt under me a bridge that I was glad they had passed over and so wouldn't burn, because I didn't know many bridges, and I liked how it felt.

"Smythe's barn's afire."

"I told you that bunch from over around Sycamore Creek'd do it soon's he went over into Kentucky to join up with our Union boys."

"Let's go git 'em!"

"Soon's we turn our backs on that bridge and it afire."

"Widder Tipton'll have to take them in. There goes her light. The smell of burnin's woke her up."

It came over me—these men know every face behind every window we pass.

"I don't *need* to go to no Kentucky. I'm where I'm supposed to be, doing just what I'm supposed to do."

"When the Union army comes, them MacPhersons will empty out from around here."

"And what'll you do, Tom? Sit across the road and stare at their house?"

"Well, ain't them Rebels hurt *us,* and drove us off, and murdered and—?"

"I ain't the one to blame you. Take it. And hope Walter MacPherson don't come back and visit you with all his Iron Mountain kin."

I imagined slaves—though I had never seen a solitary one—along the route watching us, their heads full of pictures.

"My wife snuck a chicken leg into my saddle bag."

I wanted me a bite.

"My hands and feet is freezing."

I wanted to chime in, "Mine, too!" but I feared one of my folks would recognize my voice.

As we passed a schoolhouse, one of the voices said, "I should a kept going to that school house, I reckon, but I just couldn't stand it."

The sky was the ceiling of a smoky cabin, pressing down. The forks of creeks and rivers told them where they were.

"Cover that bald, Jack," I heard my daddy tell my oldest brother, "less you want to catch cold," and I felt like *I* wasn't even there amongst them.

Mountains made us feel closed in, blackness heaped up on each side, a narrow path along a creek running between.

As we passed a church, somebody said, "Well, now I can say I been to church, can't I?"

"My momma's buried in that cemetery," my grandpa said, and I felt left out, because it was the first I heard about it.

"Now, boys," says the voice of Captain Fry, "they's a nest of Rebel houses up ahead and I mean to bypass it without notice. It's all up if they see us, so get low and hush."

"You come without a coat?" my grandpa said. "Were you born a fool, or reborn a fool yesterday? Well, have you a gun, or only a whirligig?" Until he said "whirligig," I couldn't figure out which of our people he was talking to. Bob was awful bad to while the time away whittling whirligigs to give the little chaps as Christmas play pretties.

"Don't worry bout the cold, boys. We ain't far from warm."

Something moved over yonder. A swinging bridge over a creek, wobbling. Somebody had just run across it. Or a dog. Or a wild cat.

"How'd *you* vote Wednesday?"

"Same's I'd vote every other day of the week, if I could—against ol' Devil Davis."

"Pass that jug."

"Who brought a jug, after I forbade it?" The voice of Captain Fry.

"Jug? Who said jug?"

Up under the sycamores, moonlight washed over an out-cropping of rocks, like a fortress.

"Called me a Rebel and a Secessionist till I showed him my knuckles before he saw 'em comin'!"

"Them slinging 'Torie' at me's almost as bad as sticks and stones."

"My people was at King's Mountain, and prob'ly boiled a few Tories in bear piss."

"Call me a Lincolnite, even a Yankee 'er som-bitch, but call me a Torie and see if I don't reach up your ass and snatch your heart out for you."

Swept along toward the bridge they were to burn, I heard my mother's voice, spelling out the Rebel cause. She would pull me off away from the men and their Union talk and beg me to side with her and her people down in the town. She never lived Mountain life with any feeling for it. "God forbid, but the time may come when you will be forced to choose the Confederacy or the Union." Before that day came, I hoped I would see clear which was which. *Why* seemed even darker.

To rest, they chose Mountain crests, where, eating and drinking, we looked back, down over Elizabethton, and valleys, cabin lights, widely separate, showing where we would ride directly. Such sights made me feel bold, like when we hunted, and from high up, I would suddenly see off into eternity. But I had to keep hid among the trees. The humiliation of that rock throwing still stung.

"Bridges was made for my own feet and my horse's hooves, not, I want you to know, for narrow railroad tracks, and a train that would push me off into the gorge, if I was walking."

"Never did like the sound of a train," said one man who must have lived close enough to hear one go by.

"Nor the sight of one roaring around the Mountain," another man joined in.

"Always hate to see that old engine go by."

The Mountains became only hills, and up ahead we saw the valley level out. Moonlight on the road was shiny as a kettle.

Then it was only a few words at a time, with miles of no talk between. At the forks of a creek and a river, I heard my grandpa's voice. "Get ready to cross over into Greene County, boys."

"This critter can smell the difference and don't want to go," my brother Tim said.

By that time, I felt shut out. I rode with them, but felt alone riding behind a man whose face I couldn't see, and never did. He could have been the moonlight turned into a phantom horseman. I wished my three brothers would turn into one brother, one who would say, "Climb up here with *me*."

"Here we walk 'em, men." Captain Fry's voice was like a stream that carried us all along. "Over that hill is a force of Rebels. Tamp your pipes and button your lips and let nothing jingle. Let them that's awake hear only the music of the spheres."

"Like to hear *that* myself," somebody whispered, hoarse.

"Then let *yours* be the last human sound," said Colonel Fry, "till we shout victory at the bridge."

Narrow and sluggish, Lick Creek runs between broad, flat, marshy meadow lands, so the bridge is long, about a mile long.

We pass under a low branch of an oak tree, forked, strong enough to hang two men.

They surrounded a tent and took seven Rebel soldiers prisoner. I hung about outside, wishing I could go in there with my grandpa and my daddy.

"Stay in this tent less you want us to roast you, too, you gap-tooth woman-killer. Stand over him, Henry."

"You bat an eye, you gonna scare my trigger-finger, turd."

"You one of them that crossed over into Kentucky with Daniel Ellis to fight with the Union?" No answer. "What you doing back here in a Rebel uniform, then?"

"Don't that anger you? Does me."

"This is richer'n I can stomach, Thomas. Changin' sides like changin' your britches. Well, piss in them, sir."

"I reckon you want us to hang you from that tree, mister. They come up the line, find you dancing a Rebel jig."

"*We* ain't setting no fire to Rebel property. It was *you* done it. Take this torch or this bullet one, Rebel."

"This ain't the way I like to spend my Friday nights—ner Saturday mornin's."

"And then have to hide out Sunday, preacher come a-looking for ye," another man whispered, hoarse.

My brother Jack looked close at me, and when he saw who I was, he told me to get home, but I could see he wasn't going to take time to hound my heels out of sight.

"How's that wire do what it does?" I asked a man who was fixing to climb a telegraph pole.

"Ask them that does it. Anything nature, ask *me*, boy."

"What's that nigger up to?" I heard Jack ask.

"He wants to help us do it."

I had never laid eyes on a slave, so I rushed around in the dark, eager to take a look at him.

"I'd soon not include slaves in this," said Captain Fry, even though these were all Union raiders.

My first slave was gone before I could locate him.

"Some of them will betray you, wanting immediate favor with their master more than to risk freedom for the rest of their lives."

"'Force the gates of hell, men!'"

"Heap on the brush, then you can put the torch to it."

"This old rotten wood's dry enough to fire, if Brownlow'd breathe on it."

"Burn that wood bin."

"Want me to fire this water tank?"

I'd never seen one before.

"No. The bridge burns everything with it."

"That ain't no bridge. That's a Union bygod *altar*!"

"I consecrate this fire," somebody said, like a preacher, "to freedom in East Tennessee."

"Fine words," said Captain Fry, "got us *in* this war."

"I got wet."

"We're *all* wet."

"Can't I just turn my butt to the fire a while longer?"

"If you want to hang around, them Rebels'll 'blige you."

"And you had the stars and stripes inside your coat the whole time?"

"Fooled you, didn't I? Ain't it pretty? Joe, throw this Rebel rag in the fire."

"Sounds like a Methodist camp meetin'!"

"Hey, men, I suspicion a Baptist among us!"

Captain Fry returned to the tent with a large number of men and cursed the seven guards.

"That night three months ago, you goddamn men, or men of your sentiments, ran me out of Greene County, but now, I have you under my thumb and will do with you as I please. Within the past week, I've been all over this railroad, from Chattanooga to Bristol."

That struck me a strange way to use up two weeks, but of course I didn't open my trap.

"Jeff Davis and South Carolina cotton men have had possession of this railroad long enough. We're taking it over and using it ourselves. A whole Union regiment besides the cavalry is in Knoxville right now, ready to rout every one of you son-of-a-bitchin' secessionists from the region. You have the choice of taking an oath never to take up arms against the United States government or to die right here and now, immediately."

"How does the oath go?"

The seven Rebel soldiers took it.

"Take down each man's name."

"'The names will be given!'" I mimicked, but everybody seemed deaf to it.

A raider, sheathing his knife, went into the tent, declaring, "Well, Colonel Fry, that damned wire's done telling on us now."

"My clothes caught afire!" I turned and saw a man on a horse, about to go up in smoke.

"Grab his horse!"

"It's spooked!"

Horse and rider lit off running into the fire.

Somebody yelled, "Say that piece again, Ed!"

"Don't need to—we done did it."

But not soon enough. Through Bull's Gap came a Union troop train almost exploding with fire over the burning bridge, knocking the burning raider and his panicked horse over the side, its cars trailing smoke as it kept on in the direction of Elizabethton.

They burned that bridge from bank to bank.

"That train will carry no more Unionist prisoners to Montgomery."

Three hours later, we were deep in the Mountains again, the smell of smoke and tar still in our dirty clothes, and the heat and smell of the campfire made the burning of the bridge over Lick Creek seem as if we were still in the very midst of it.

When the bear meat got done and we were carving it and handing it around, smoking on a wood plank, several of them told the whole story over again, even though all of us had been there, and each told it a different way. And now me.

My daddy said the Rebels would hunt us down, and they were all going to get Daniel Ellis to pilot them over into Kentucky to join up with General Thomas and the other East Tennessee Unionists, and so I must go back home and take care of the women, children, and old folks, like they told me to start with. So they chased me off again.

But I hid close by, scalded that they still treated me like a kid, instead of a thirteen-year-old that strangers took for a man of nineteen.

Union troops caught up with us, killed some, wounded and captured my brother Tim and some others, while the rest scattered and got away.

By the time I figured out what was what, everybody was gone. Bridge-burners now, fugitives from Confederate law, gone off to find the War and fight for the Union.

I said to myself, I'll look for the War on my lonesome. Knoxville, that's probably where they got that War.

"Castle Fox" Prison

SINCE PARSON BROWNLOW BUCKSHOT ALL THOSE WORDS ABOUT THE War out of Knoxville, I figured a big part of the War must be going on there, Rebels on one side of town and Yankees on the other, the way folks on the north side of Holston Mountain were nothing like us Carrs on our side.

When I asked a fellow down about Greeneville, "Sir, how far does this road go?" he said, "All the way to the end, boy."

All the way to Knoxville and during all that long time it took me to get there, I was hurt and wrathful that my brother Tim was wounded and captured.

On a street wide as a river that runs down the middle of Knoxville, I asked somebody who looked neutral, "Which way is the Unionists?"

He said, "Young'un, come with *me. I'll* show you where we got some Union boys."

He took me down the street, back towards the river, took me in some old building, took me down into the basement, and there were a hundred men laying around, shoved up against each other, looking sick.

"Get in there with *them* people, where you belong!" he said, and back of him stood three or four soldiers in blue, grinning like they were making fun of me.

They had clapped me into prison, named "Castle Fox" after its jailor.

Men were dying, and seeing so many grown men scared to death got me scared, too. I looked all around for Tim. Then I looked again for anybody in the gang that burned the bridge, but except for the firelight, I had never seen their faces up close.

Thirsty from hiking it down the pike all day, I asked for water, and several pointed weakly at a solitary bucket. It looked like slop water, so I turned my back on it. I saw not a single solitary bench, chair, or stool.

They kept bringing people in who were to go to prison in Tuscaloosa for being Unionists like us Carrs, and I got the picture: in the city of Knoxville, it was mostly Rebels, while us Unionists were mostly spread out over the hills and Mountains of East Tennessee. The war itself was off in other places.

I listened to prisoners tell many tales about the burning of the bridge. No two told it the same way. Myself, I kept mum.

Everybody was so sad, loping around and moping around, when suddenly the doors flung open, the guards stood aside, and in walked this old man. He walked in with his head up, and he had fire in his eyes, and the entire population greeted him as if he were Our Savior, or at least a prince of the realm.

I thought, Who in the world is *that* man? He's gonna turn us all loose or something. Somebody who looks like that.

When a fellow told me, "Why, that's Parson Brownlow," I calmed down. Now it was like sleeping in the loft, knowing Greatgrandfather Carr was sitting by "the place of fire."

Parson Brownlow came up out of a fit of coughing, and in a hoarse voice proclaimed, "This is the proudest day of my life! And none of you people should be sad here tonight, for you die in a great cause!"

And he would raise his arms and he would raise his voice and he would lower his voice and he would reach up and dip down and he would go among them and touch them and he had them all pacified and then he had them all fired up and then he had them all proud, and when he had them all the way he wanted them, *he* laid down and went to sleep.

I threaded my way in among the men to get nearer to him.

"The meanest man to walk the streets of Knoxville, *some* of 'em say," one man told the Rebel guard by the door. "That vile serpent Brownlow, some of 'em say. The ugliest man to come out of East Tennessee— Brownlow himself says."

"A voice forged in hell, *we* say," said the guard, then pounded the butt of his rifle on the floor.

It went around the big room that they had arrested the Parson for inciting the burning of the bridges.

What bridges? I wondered. It was only one bridge. But I kept my trap shut.

Somebody told me they had heard that my brother Tim had been sent on the cars to Tuscaloosa, but another man said he thought they had hung him down by the river. I couldn't find out for certain what.

Roadweary, I did go to sleep but nightmares kept me wakeful. Somebody cried out for his Momma, but I couldn't swear it was me.

"Here comes Dick the Waterboy!" somebody yelled, looking out the basement window.

I felt like talking to somebody near by own age, so I meandered over to the window, but Dick the Waterboy had already pushed his wagon past the window.

"You at the winder!" a guard said. "Go fetch the water for these Unionist scum!"

"That's *you,* boy," the man at the window beside me said. "Jump to it, we're all sick of drinking out of that bucket, for the damn guards have washed their socks in it."

A guard took me by the collar and handed me a bucket and danced me outside. Me, because I'm a boy, I thought, resentful, then remembered I was being taken, as usual, for a young man.

The water bucket set on the steps outside but Dick the Waterboy was almost out of sight, and his bent back made me wonder how old he was, so I asked the guard, and he said, "Oh, he's just Dick, the old nigger water boy, that's all."

Soon as I set the water bucket down in the midst of all those men, one of the guards spit in it before the first man got hold of the dipper.

And the Rebel officers came in and yelled, "All right! you! and you! and you!"

And I asked, "What's that for?"

And a man said, "They taking some out to go on the cars to Alabama and some they gonna hang, for burning them bridges."

And I heard a man telling that they had already hung three of them over the railroad track at Lick Creek, where people passing slowly in the train could stand on the rear platform and reach out with sticks and beat them, until after four days their corpses stunk so bad, the commander had to cut them down.

"When we get out of here, let's track down the Rebel officer who did this."

"Let the names be given!" Parson Brownlow came up out of his sleep, his finger rising over his head.

"Colonel Leadbetter!" rose like a chorus.

The next afternoon, Parson Brownlow was writing in a little book and several men were craning their necks to see.

"What's that you writin' all the time?" one of them finally asked, though timidly.

"A record of infamy for the judgment day! It's all here! What my own ears have heard and my own eyes have seen! All the Unionist sufferings! I shall commit it all to print the day I am released from this Rebel dungeon."

"Read it out so we can all hear it *now*, Parson."

Without hesitating, he flipped the pages backward and commenced to read. "'One day, these fiends came to the jail with two carts and took Old Harmon, a Methodist class leader, and his son.'" As I listened to his voice, injured from years ago by too much loud preaching in the cold Mountain air, sometimes soakin' wet from swimming a Mountain stream, and made worse recently from sleeping in Wear's Cove up in the Smokies where he had been hiding, I imagined Greatgrandfather reading it aloud up on the Mountain. "'Old Mr. Harmon was seated in one cart upon his coffin, and his son in the other, and each cart was surrounded by a strong guard of Rebel bayonets and driven down the hill to a scaffold in sight of the jail. The young man was hung first, and the father was compelled to look upon his death struggles. Then he was told to mount the scaffold, but as he was feeble and overpowered by his feelings, two of the ruffians took hold of him, one of them saying, 'Get up there, you damned old traitor!' and the poor old man was launched into Eternity after his son.

"'A few days after this, they came up to the jail with another cart, and took away a young man, an excellent young man of fine morals and good common sense.'"

Tim? I wondered.

"'He had a wife and two children. He was informed only one hour beforehand that he was to be hung. He immediately asked for a Methodist preacher who lives in Knoxville to come to see him and to pray with him. They said to him, 'We don't permit any praying for a damned Union-shrieker.'

"'He met his fate like a man. When under the scaffold, a drunken, lying chaplain rose up and delivered a short address. Said he, 'The poor, unfortunate young man, who is now about to pay the penalty for his crimes, says that he regrets his course, and that he was led into it through the influence of traitors like that vile serpent Brownlow. He is, therefore, deserving of your pity.'

"'As quick as thought, the young man sprang to his feet and, in a much stronger and steadier tone than the lying villain beside him had made use of, said, 'My fellow citizens, there is not one word of truth in what that man has told you. I have made no such concession. On the contrary, all that I have said and done, I have said and done after mature deliberation, and I would do the same again. I am here ready to be executed.'"

I wanted to ask Parson Brownlow, Was he already wounded? But I reckon I was tongue-tied.

"'He died as every Union man ought to die when called to face death by villains and traitors.'"

"Like the man says, 'A voice forced in hell!'" I heard a guard declare. "He ought to be vomited out of the Confederacy!"

And one morning, a Rebel officer came in, looked me right in the eye, and said, "Well, young'un, you want to go with these people we putting on the train to Tuscaloosa?"

Hell, no, I thought, but only shook my head.

"Well, then, you got your choice. You want to fight in the Rebel army with *us,* or do you want to go to Tuscaloosa?" The very name sounded like the end of everything holy.

And I thought, These people are dumber than hell. They are too dumb to know that as soon as I get out of here in *their* army, I'm gonna light out for the Union side, because my daddy said that's where I *ought* to be. And I'll probably find some of my people over there, too.

So I said, "Yeah, I'll be a Rebel soldier."

And the prisoners all jeered and cursed me as I stepped over and among them to get out of there, but at the door, I turned and winked, the way my big brother Jack always winked to tease you, make you guess what he meant to do.

"Son, You Got the Eye for It!"

AT DAWN, THEY PUT A UNIFORM ON ME, THEY PUT ME ON A TRAIN, THEY put me in a camp, and that was good. Camp fires, bacon grease, and wood smoke, and coffee pots clanking on stones made me begin to feel settled, like camping up on Holston with my grandpa and my daddy and my brothers, and I enjoyed that, just sitting around, some of those fellows from up around Elizabethton, and I got to liking *that*.

Then somebody pointed out our general. "There goes Ol' Pete."

I was with General Longstreet in the Peninsula Campaign, but that was only a name to me. So was Fort Sumter when men would say the first shot was fired upon it. When they talked about "Manassas," what I heard was "molasses," and wanted some. And I thought Bull Run was a separate battle, not the same one with two names, given by the two sides. The South favored towns, like Manassas, but for the North, it was rivers, like Bull Run.

One day I was shooting at tin cans—and hitting each one.

As I was reloading, a voice behind me said, "Son, you got the eye for it!"

And I said, "For what?" turning around.

It was our captain. "To be a Sharpshooter."

That sounded good to me. A *Sharpshooter*. Yes, that's *me*. A *Sharpshooter*. All right, I'll desert tomorrow or the next day. I'll see what this sharpshooting is like. And what I saw it was like was, it was good, it made me feel good, and everybody was proud of me, everybody looked up to me, and I was only thirteen years old.

The first time I looked through a telescopic sight and fixed the brow of a Yankee officer in the cross-hairs, I broke the firm resolve I had held up to then to desert to the Yankees. I shot him. I killed him. Maybe I was sorry. I disremember.

Sharpshooter. That's what I was. Sharp, I thought, meant me—keen, clear. When I learned that what gave me my name was not a quality in my character but the rifle itself, which I learned still later was named for a man named Christian Sharps, I was a little befuddled. I was also called a sniper. But I knew what a snipe bird was, and I wasn't a snipe.

I quickly enjoyed the fact that Sharpshooters were privileged characters. We moved at will or on special orders. The infantry always shot at the privates because they were trying to shoot *them*. But the Sharpshooters scanned the ranks for the officers and picked off the artillerymen. We were often resented as aristocrats are.

And so I went with *them*.

And I *stayed* with them. With General Longstreet. I was at Gettysburg with him. I was with him until I found myself up in a burning tree in the Wilderness.

Sharpshooting for General Longstreet

I WAS AT GAINE'S MILL BUT I COULDN'T TELL YOU MUCH ABOUT IT IF YOU promised to shoot me. I was in battles by many mills. The strange name Savage Station stuck, but only the name. Frayser's Farm. After Malvern Hill, the phrase "It was not war—it was murder" comes to mind, but not who said it. And the phrase "Seven Pines" covers all those battles of the summer of '62.

I recall a long march, a battle at Thoroughfare Gap, to join with General Stonewall Jackson at what turned out to be First Manassas for me, Second Manassas for General Jackson and others. I recall an old railroad embankment. An old stone house. A repaired stone bridge.

About a month later, we crossed the Potomac River into Maryland. A Sharpshooter at Sharpsburg—not likely to forget that. Shot some officers and artillerymen, I suppose. Dead lay in the grass in front of a squat white church. Horse carcasses all around a white house. A cornfield full of dead. A sunken road called Bloody Lane.

At Fredericksburg, Rebels and Yankees organized a big snowball fight, and somebody woke me, saying, "Merry Christmas."

I, with some others, was attached for a while to Barksdale's Mississippi Sharpshooters, or "Confederate Hornets," as General Longstreet called them, to stop the Yankees from laying a pontoon bridge across the Rappahanock. Despite artillery fire from the bluffs across the river, we held them off for a long time.

One day, I came down out of a church tower during a truce to see what the Mississippians were doing, bunched up on our side of the destroyed railroad bridge, looking out over the river.

They were posing for a Yankee photographer and a man was sketching them from the other side. I thought, "These men are full of beans," and went back up in the tower to wait for the truce to end.

Our boys shouted across the Rappahanock, "Before you get to Richmond, you got a Longstreet to travel, a big Hill to climb, and a 'Stonewall' to get over!"

From the church tower, I watched a giant balloon float over.

Finally, the Yankees got across the Rappahanock and drove us back through the burning town and we Sharpshooters joined the infantrymen behind the stone wall on the sunken road up on Marye's Heights. As they charged us across the vast open field, we killed a great many of them.

There was a lone little old house to our left. Everybody who tells about the War seems to remember a house—large or small—at each battle. It was white before the charge, but by the end, bullets had scraped it down to rough red brick. A black, cast iron stove leaned against the house. Bullets struck different notes on it.

The general we opposed there at Fredericksburg was Burnside. The name always made me see a man jumping up and down with a burn on his ass.

The accidental shooting of Stonewall Jackson by his own men during the battle of Chancellorsville and what they told us he said as he was dying, "Let us cross over the river and rest in the shade of the trees," made me think that we were there, too. But, no, we were down at Suffolk, and somewhere else, a Yankee officer across a river rose up and exposed himself to taunt us. "Why don't you south'ron gentlemen cross over the river and rest in the shade of the trees." I never laid eyes on Jackson himself, but I did that officer, as clearly as I needed to.

I hear hundreds of North Carolina men have special reason to mourn Stonewall Jackson to this day, for each of them thinks it was he who accidentally shot him.

At Gettysburg, I was in awe of the massive Gateway to the Public Cemetery. Seminary Ridge and Cemetery Ridge sounded the same to my ears and I thought they were. Big Round Top and Little Round Top. Pickett's Charge, that I watched from a distance. I operated out of Devil's Den and lived to tell it.

And lived to ride the train the long way south to Chattanooga. That was in the early fall of 1863, my second year in the war. Bragg was facing Grant. "Send up Longstreet." General Lee detached him, and they put us on the cars, and we went West. We came to the rescue, making the crucial breakthrough in the Union line at Chickamauga. The battle was already going when we crossed Alexander's Bridge and made the difference. We felt pretty good about that.

That's where I first heard about—or really listened to the talk about—General Nathan Bedford Forrest, who was always out front of his men on a white horse, that somebody shot out from under him at Alexander's Bridge. I always wanted to see him in person. I don't know why. Maybe it was because I always had the feeling he was out there by his lonesome.

The Yankees retreated into Chattanooga and we put the city under siege. We held Missionary Ridge to the south, Lookout Mountain to the west, and our batteries and we Sharpshooters kept them off the Tennessee River. October rains kept them off the roads, and General Forrest burned the railroad bridges. So they told me.

Then, Bragg didn't like having a man like General Longstreet around, so he says, "Burnside has taken Knoxville. Why don't you go up there and run him out?"

So they put us on the cars again, and we got as far as Sweetwater, where the railroad was all knocked out, and so we started marching—in the rain and sleet, November, cold, no shoes.

We passed a cabin that reminded me of ours up on the Mountain, and I remembered Greatgrandfather stirring fire up out of ashes that I took for dead.

Fever Dream in Bleak House Tower

I HAD A FEVER FROM MARCHING THROUGH THE MUD AND RAIN AND COLD, and didn't quite know what was going on, I was barefoot, most of us were barefoot.

Now, a Sharpshooter can go wherever he wants to, he's a free man, that's part of it. So you just naturally gravitate to high places. I saw a house on a hill, highest hill, the highest house, I saw the tower up there, I didn't even *think* about it, I just went on through, past a man who was painting a scene on the wall, smelled the paint, and I climbed that staircase, and two came behind me.

Near the top of the ladder, I looked around the floor, at eye-level. As my body rose into the tower, I looked through a window in front of me into the tops of trees without leaves. Pausing, one foot on the tower floor, one foot on the top step, I looked around, through a window to the left, out into darkness, and then I looked to my right and saw yet a third window. That was so strange, in a room not much larger than a wagon bed, that I began to see more clearly—two tall, slender windows, each divided into sections of beveled glass, filled each of three brick walls. I put both feet on the floor, holding my rifle, deliberately did a smart about face so I could see the complete window pattern, but the West wall was blind.

The other two Sharpshooters came up close behind me, one of them with shoes, the strings tied together, dangling off his shoulder, the other gobbling some pone. He gave me a chunk, and I slumped down on the floor, my back against the narrow space between the windows in the east wall, soaking wet from days and nights of rain on the long march from Sweetwater.

We settled into our new Sharpshooter's nest.

Below the tower, in the music room that I had glimpsed as we came in, General Longstreet walked in his boots and sometimes raised his voice, a drone or a boom like distant thunder, or like artillery that sometimes sounded like thunder, setting the chandeliers vibrating.

The sun, pouring through my windows, woke me, only an hour after I had fallen asleep. Looking out from this tower room was a little like looking out of my own cabin door—we had no windows in the cabin. The house set on a bluff by the river and the tower was on top of two high stories.

I stood at each of the tall, slender, round-topped windows, like church windows, but clear, not stained, and looked out north, south, east.

From up there, I could look all around, down on the Tennessee River, down on the pike that had brought us here and would, we hoped, take us on into Knoxville. All the way to the end, as the fellow said.

Between futile artillery assaults on the house, I slept in my damp clothes in the cold tower, where during the early morning and that day, I worked up a chest cold.

I watched a few Yankees now and then leave their position behind the piles of fence rails, their only cover on that bare hill, and begin to fade backward in retreat.

Then an officer would appear on the crest of the hill, half his tall frame erect above the rails, exposing himself to our fire at close range until every retreating man returned to his proper place, knowing their officer would then take cover, too.

In the tower now, in addition to the two who had come up with me, were seven more Sharpshooters, but when a ball hit just below, the seven new Sharpshooters got out of there and on out of the house and scattered.

The Sharpshooter from Virginia, who was only two years older than I was, fired from one of the tower's east windows. "I got him," he said, the way you do when your target is somebody special. Too feverish to focus, I had stopped firing, clenching my eyes, breathing deeply of the raw November air that whistled through bullet holes in the thick beveled window panes to clear my head, spent Minié balls all around, my feet sticking straight out in front of me like a doll's propped in a corner. The two previously wounded men were half asleep, moaning. I was idly watching the Virginian when I began intentionally watching him, the look of his shoulders declaring that he was taking very, very careful aim—an even more exceptional target. As if to help him see through the telescopic lens more keenly, I held my own breath, and waited for him to say, "I got him." As I stared at him, a suffocating feeling beginning to rise from my chest to swell my head and blur my vision, I saw a narrow stream of blood appear between his knees where he knelt and move toward where I sat against the blind West wall.

So I thought, well, I'll see what's going on out there, and I crawled across the tower floor to the narrow window beside the Virginian and looked out at the bare hillside that rose across the Kingston road, eastward.

An officer on a white horse rode back and forth in front of the fence rails, *charging* back and forth in front of the Yankees that was firing at us. He was going back and forth like he was daring us to kill him. Shoot! Shoot! I'm here! See if you can *do* it! Riding back and forth. And when he passed the lone cedar tree, my feverish heart leapt at the magnificence of what I took to be an image of my fever, for he had no business in the real war, being where he was, doing what he was doing. He was too foolhardy to be one of *our* officers riding ahead of the infantry toward the rails, exhorting his men. Nobody, on our side or their side, is crazy enough to be doing what I'm watching, it's fever, it's fever. He had to be my own contribution, an optical illusion my own feelings conjured to fit this occasion. Not to determine whether he was a romantic vision instead of an actual heroic figure but to hold onto the sight that so lifted my spirits, I reached for my own rifle. I was so wobbly, it took me a while to get him in my telescopic sights, but I got him, and I followed him as he rode toward the lone cedar tree again. My, my, I can just shoot at that fellow and it won't even hurt him. That's kind of nice, shoot somebody that you can see plain as a brass knob, know it's fever, shoot at him, won't even hurt him. Exhausted, confused, feverish, knowing it wouldn't kill, I impulsively pulled the trigger, and I just turned away, I didn't even see if I *got* him. I lowered the rifle, thinking, well, my stray bullet may accidentally hit one of the Yankees behind the fence rails. I crawled back to the West wall and leaned against the cold brick, and looked into the wide open eyes of one of the wounded men who seemed to have been watching my odd behavior.

"Did you get him?"

I smiled, closing my eyes, thinking, he is in so much pain, he doesn't even know the Virginian is dead.

"I brought you boys some hot coffee and pone," said a head on a level with the floor, the sound of a man who had repeated what he had said for the third time. He climbed on up into the tower.

He was sorry to discover the dead Virginian and the two wounded men. "We thought all of you cleared out of here when that ball hit the house, but one of them came back to the house while we were eating and said he thought you and one or two others were still up here. I'll go get help and get you boys out of here."

But he didn't come back right away, and when I had finished eating mine and was staring at the north wall where the sun struck, something about the look of the light on the plaster made me want to stop everything in the tower at this moment, before anybody came up to disturb what I saw. The wounded men were dozing in agony, their heads still. On the wall, I began to draw, with a pencil I had taken off a dead Yankee and that I rented out to soldiers who could write, the face of one of the wounded men, his mouth open in agony, a very small profile, and as I drew from memory the face of the dead man, who still knelt with his back to me, a feeling of power surged through me, and then I drew the other wounded man, and drew the first wounded man again, the largest of the three heads—they seemed to get bigger as I felt my strength from the hot pone and the act of drawing grow. Then I noticed that in drawing the first man again, I had enclosed upon his forehead my first tiny sketch of his profile. The first man had a mustache and goatee, the second wounded man had a beard. I noticed later that all their eyes looked exactly the same in my drawings. And after soldiers came up and had taken the two wounded men down, screaming because the awkward descent hurt, and lifted the Virginia Sharpshooter off his knees and laid him out on his back, I saw that the face I had drawn was even younger than his and did not resemble his but that of someone more familiar, one of my brothers maybe or myself.

"He's as heavy as a horse," one of the men said, as they started down the narrow steps with the Virginian's corpse.

I saw that they had not smudged the bloodstain on the wall and the floor. It looked like the drippings from a brush.

A little while later, the man who had brought the hot coffee and the pone stuck his head up again and looked at me along the floor. He set a bucket up on the floor and a rag.

"General Longstreet is very upset over the death of the boy. He was his favorite Sharpshooter. He told me to tell you to clean up the blood."

I shook my head, no, with no hesitation.

He tried it again, and I mechanically repeated my answer. And a third time. Then he climbed up and did what I knew all along the general had told *him* to do, because the idea of Sharpshooters being exempt from such work, from anything but finding a place and pulling a trigger, was *his*. But I had no intention of doing it even if General Longstreet had ordered it. I wanted nothing disturbed, nothing changed.

I asked the man to write "Men who were shot up here" under my drawings of the men, because nobody had yet taught me how to write. He had to read each word aloud to me three times, because I wanted to be sure.

An hour later, the man took up his empty bucket and his sopping rag and went back down, and I looked at the perfect dripping of blood, as clear as before, on the wall under the window and on the floor, and I looked at the three heads I had drawn, the tiny fourth head in the middle of the forehead of the face on the right.

I crawled over there and drew arrows from the words pointing up at each head.

Then I sat back in the middle of the floor, the stairwell at my back, and stared at the faces until the light got too bad.

General Longstreet buried, mourned the boy Sharpshooter from Virginia.

He had taken no notice of me. And now that I was sick, I was allowed to sleep in the tower, on call.

So I stayed at my post, a deadly observer, alone, able to see and fire from any of the six little windows in the three sides of the tower.

I was now too far behind our lines to get hit. Free to look or lie down in peace.

To the south rose the ranges of the Great Smoky Mountains. They reminded me of South Holston, except that it felt odd to realize that I had never seen our own Mountain at a distance like that.

When the time comes, I will get down out of the tower and look for a place where I can do the most damage.

All day long I heard both Union and Confederate bands play, and watched gangs of slaves haul cotton bales, covered with rawhide so rifle fire won't ignite them, into a Union fort a mile away to build up the parapets.

The Yankees occupied all the houses facing west, and when they pulled back, they burned them, probably because they obstructed the fire of Yankee guns.

And further north, fires cast a dazzling light against the cold night sky and over the fields and into the forest, and an explosion louder than any cannon woke me.

Rain dampened firing along the picket line and made the ashes of the house fires sodden, sending up a great canopy of wood smoke and mist.

I wondered when the assault would start. In the morning, it was so fiercely cold and foggy neither side could have seen each other to open with a cannonade.

At noon the sun was bright and I watched through my telescopic lens General Longstreet and his aides ride out to the hill to survey the situation and watched them ride back.

From the tower, I saw horses, lying on their sides as if asleep (when they looked dead, I used to call to them on the lower slopes of Holston Mountain, where farmers left them to graze, glad when they jumped up), or their legs flexed, stiff, to kick heaven. I watched soldiers with hooks on long poles pull Yankee dead horses floating down the Tennessee River over to the bank and yank their shoes off, as I had watched soldiers on every river do.

Almost every evening, I watched the men play hide and seek barefooted in the biting cold, Yankees and Rebels together.

In the tower above General Longstreet's headquarters, I was like a deserter. I sneaked down in the dead of night for food.

I saw Sharpshooters taking positions.

As our men began to move out of the house, I felt forgotten and knew that I could stay where I was, that I could desert simply by not moving.

When I came down out of the tower, I looked, as a free agent, for a place where I could do the most harm to officers and artillerymen.

The Battle of Fort Sanders in a Sharpshooter's Sights

As I joined one of the Sharpshooters, he pointed to a fort. "The order came down that the attack will begin in darkness, just before sunrise."

As we Sharpshooters advanced to the enemy lines during the night, to be in position to hold down fire from the fort during our assault, Roman candles exploded over the field. Some of the shells were very different from any I had seen before—three separate explosions out of each.

Sleet and rain swept over us.

Our orders were to keep up a steady fire into the fort to restrict cannon fire and rifle fire as our brigades attacked. That was what we usually did, everywhere else we had been, and the layout of this fort was familiar.

That night, a chilling mist hung over us. Forbidden fires, we lay on our arms and suffered the cold awfully.

I wished I was back up in the tower.

At 6 o'clock, I saw our signalman swing a low-lit lantern.

I heard our signal gun fire near the house where I had left the tower. I heard our battery on the south side of the river fire.

I heard our battery north, across the railroad, fire. With about a hundred other Sharpshooters, I fired on the parapet. From the fort above, no guns fired.

But from a hill to the east, Yankee guns fired at our battery on the bluff across the river.

Steam poured out of the embrasures in the parapet of the fort and water streamed down the embankment, a sight I had never seen before.

I watched our support move up from the rear, closer to the attack column, and I supposed the commander had realized he had stopped too far back to be effective.

The cannonading stopped, and our men, as if borne upon the Rebel yell, rushed forward, past us Sharpshooters.

Our men hit the brush barriers that I had slipped through the night before, pushed them aside, but I saw some of them fall on the sharp stobs that were sticking up out of the ground and I saw more of them trip in the dark over wires woven among the stumps that I had mistaken in the night for vines, because telegraph wire had never been used before.

Men surging up from behind fell over the men who had tripped in the web of wires.

One cannon in the fort fired two fast rounds of canister into the tangle of bodies.

When they exposed themselves on the platform, I tried to kill the gunners, but failed.

As our men quickly closed ranks and charged toward the ditch, the union gunners ran out of the ditch into the fort.

Our men reached the ditch. They discovered too late that it was not *four* feet deep, as they had been told, it was, in some places, *eleven* feet deep! On that inspection tour I had observed, our own General Longstreet had misjudged.

Past experience made them expect to be able to get a toehold on what was called the berme and to scale the parapet in a single leap. But the Yankees had cut the berme away, so that our men were shocked at how steep it was.

The men followed furrows of plowed ground for easier movement but converged together in confusion and curses. Only trick furrows could converge that way. Out of that confusion, officers could not regroup their own men.

The embankment was slippery with ice, a solid sheet, still smoking. That was what the steam had been—the Yankees had poured scalding water down the embankments, knowing it would turn into a wall of smoking ice.

The men crowded together in the ditch. Some fired into the embrasures and at any Yankee who showed a silhouette above. That is what I was doing too.

A Yankee above yelled, "Pick off the officers! Pick off the officers!" turned and started to shout a third time, but I sent a bullet into the back of his head and he fell down into the fort.

One of our officers tried to direct his men to attack the breastworks that led away from the fort. When his men couldn't hear him and he climbed up the ditch to command attention, a bullet instantly cut him down.

In that blind area of the ditch, the fort's cannon could not shatter the men who were trapped there.

The Yankees on the parapet were afraid to position themselves for direct firing. Several raised their muskets up above the parapet, pointed them down into the ditch, and fired without aiming.

Our guns across the river on the bluffs stopped. I wondered why.

We were unable to move forward—we were unwilling to retreat—we were paralyzed.

Because the pioneers had not been sent ahead under Sharpshooter protection with shovels and picks as was usual in such an attack, some officers and men hacked footholds in the icy red clay with swords and bayonets and attempted to climb out of the ditch. One did, and entered the fort through an embrasure. We did not see him again.

Some of the men crossed the ditch on each other's shoulders and attempted to climb the bank.

A standard-bearer ran up, in full view of the Yankees, and planted our flag upon the parapet. Shot through the heart, he fell forward into the fort.

The standard-bearer's action inspired a white-haired old colonel who shouted fiercely and led a charge up the icy bank. The old man was waving his sword and exhorting his men to follow him when a bullet knocked him sprawling. Several of his men fell around him, shot. The survivors slipped back down into the bloody ditch out of range.

And I was a Sharpshooter, just watching all that, wishing I was back up in that tower, aiming at a horseman in a fever dream.

I was able to see quickly and clearly that the lack of scaling ladders had made the men in the deep, deep ditch useless.

Time-fused shells, thrown over the parapet, killed and wounded more of our men crowded in the mire of the ditch than any other weapon. The thrashing panic I saw in that ditch made my scalp burn. As some of our men scrambled to get out of the ditch and retreat, an officer, lighting a fuse with his cigar, hollered, "Look out down there, some of you will get hurt!" I got him in my sights, just as he ducked.

"It's our own artillery shelling us!" some of our men yelled, mistaken.

Our guns stopped. General Longstreet, too, must have thought the Yankee devices were our own guns firing into the ditch where our men were trapped.

Our officers kept up the assault, but finally had to retreat.

The men falling back through the Sharpshooter's positions yelled a common plea, "Give us ladders and we will *take* the damn place!"

As the support column watched our men retreat, they, ignorant of the conditions ahead, dashed forward into the ditch to finish the assault.

Despite cannon and rifle fire from the fort, many of them reached the bank.

Then I watched everything that had happened to the first assault column happen all over again to *those* men.

They too planted flags on the parapet, and within seconds the Yankees tore them down.

Yankee officers hacked us with swords, soldiers clubbed our men with muskets, thrust bayonets, swung axes and cannon rammers. Our men kept falling back into the crowded ditch.

Yankees started coming out of the embrasures, charging our men, who were without leaders, and chased us down the ditch, capturing about two hundred of us, and driving us into the fort, a squad of Yankees following, bearing two of our battle flags, despite my aim.

Our massed assault was in shambles, but men confronted each other in fist fights, kicking, eye-gouging, screaming insults and curses.

One of our men tried to smother a shell with red clay before it could explode. It blew him into three pieces.

There was enough early light now for the enemy infantry in the trenches east and south of the fort to fire more accurately at those of our men who were still outside the ditch moving eastward and southward away from the northwest bastion that had been our point of attack. The enemy had placed cannon in such a way as to enfilade those of our men who had not yet gone down into the ditch.

The wounded started limping back through the Sharpshooter's positions. Survivors carried some of the wounded on their shoulders.

As our men retreated, we Sharpshooters saw to it that there were few casualties in the retreat itself, firing on the enemy from the picket lines we had taken from the enemy last night, keeping them down, so that the Yankees appeared above the walls of the fort to fire only one volley into our retreating columns. Our anger at being thwarted in so many unexpected ways made such a spectacle that we figured the Yankees were afraid to pursue us.

"We didn't have a fair chance!" men yelled repeatedly. "We want another chance at that fort!"

The order came down that General Longstreet had been persuaded to try again. This time the storming columns would carry ladders, long, tied bundles of brush to roll over the wires and sharp stobs to walk over, and axes to cut footholds in the frozen bank above the ditch. Our batteries were to fire heavily on the fort, and we Sharpshooters were to keep down enemy riflemen.

A great excitement overwhelmed the fact of death and wounds and humiliation in that ditch, where many of our men lay four deep, the blood running in streams, survivors slipping in it as they tried to rise to their knees.

Then General Longstreet immediately countermanded his orders, and we were told to prepare for retreat that night.

Another Sharpshooter, who had been with me in the tower, calculated that between the first assault and the cease fire, twenty minutes had passed.

Burnside offered a thirty-minute truce so that we might care for the thousand wounded and hastily bury the three hundred dead.

The whole War seemed to me like one battle, interrupted by dreams. Or one dream interrupted by battles.

Up a Burning Tree in the Wilderness

WE DID NOT RETREAT SOUTHWEST TO REJOIN BRAGG, AFTER ALL. WE HUNG about the vicinity of Knoxville, then moved slowly east, up the Great Valley of East Tennessee, roughly paralleling the railroad.

We marched through most of December, freezing in weather worse than I had ever suffered on Holston, and hungrier than usual most of the time. We sort of settled in around Mossy Creek, but we made raids back toward Knoxville at Bean's Station, Dandridge, and as close as Blaine's station. We got the best of the Yankees every time, but we never really followed up on our victories. That was often how it was, in our part of the War, anyway, and nobody could ever say exactly why.

We kept moving toward my home, through Bull's Gap, and I gazed in wonder upon the burned railroad bridges all along the way.

When we crossed Lick Creek, I stood under the tree where they hung the bridge burners and failed to stop imagining Tim hanging there.

We settled in around Greeneville a while, the town where General Morgan was killed after he escaped from that Yankee prison in Ohio, then passed through Jonesboro, within sight of Holston Mountain, and made Bristol on the Virginia line our headquarters until spring, when we marched on over into Charlottesville.

Sometime in May, we marched into a wilderness so wild they had named a church and a tavern "Wilderness."

We were the second day into a battle, and I was up in a tree, trying to pick out a Yankee officer. Thousands of men on each side shot at each other blind because of smoke from burning vines and briars and bushes and trees mingled with smoke from guns. Burning limbs fell down on the men, and I looked down on wounded, screaming men running, some afire. I saw nobody, nobody saw me. Men fired at what they heard.

And then for a while I was able to see out over everything below, but still not well enough to shoot anybody, afraid I might shoot one of our own men.

I watched General Longstreet, riding with some of his officers, disappear into a shifting wall of smoke.

A few minutes later, somebody yelled up the tree out of this sickening fog, "We have shot General Longstreet! Old Pete!"

"*We* have shot General Longstreet? What do you mean *we* have shot him?"

"One of our own men mistook and shot him in the throat."

And as I looked out over everything, it was as if, for a moment, I was still up in the tower of Bleak House, and General Longstreet is walking in his boots down below me in the music room, and his voice is a drone or a boom, like distance thunder or artillery, resounding in the great white dome of his forehead, and sometimes, walking and talking, he sets the chandeliers vibrating so I can hear them chime up in the tower.

And then all I saw was a blur and I heard nothing and got dizzyheaded. My feet on the ground, I looked up and saw my tree was afire.

I saw Ol' Pete sitting propped up against a tree, for a moment only, because the ambulance rolled up between me and him. Somebody said, "General Longstreet has crossed over the river to rest in the shade of the trees," and I remembered that a few miles from here was the place where Stonewall Jackson had fallen, he, too, shot by his own men, almost a year ago.

And I said, "Willis Carr, it's time you went home."

Walking away from the War, I had a pretty clear notion about how to hike back into East Tennessee the way we had marched into the Wilderness and find my way to our Mountain in Carter County.

I was afraid they would come looking for me. That was all right as long as I was in the vicinity of the Wilderness, because I could claim I was lost or a straggler, but when I knew I had gone so far that I rated as a deserter, I kept on old Indian paths.

And somehow I did get lost.

When it looked like I was pretty deep into Yankee-held territory, I figured I had better become a Yankee, so I shot a stray one, or maybe a deserter like me, and shucked off his uniform.

From the Guard Tower at Andersonville Prison

BUT THEN, SOMEWHERE DOWN IN GEORGIA, A REBEL PATROL JUMPED ME.

They took me to a prison just outside Andersonville. I had never seen a military prison before, but I expected to go into a place like "Castle Fox" in Knoxville.

It was not—it was far, far worse than any nightmare, or any battle, could have prepared me for. It was an open stockade, an open sewer, an open sore, a gaping wound, a log wall around a vast plot of sloping ground, not a single tree, full of shebangs and tents made of shirts, with a muddy stream crooking athwart the middle of a swamp. The sight of so many thousands of sick and starving and dead men, under a blazing sun, their uniforms so dirty and nasty they hardly resembled the one I wore, made me almost puke.

I looked for a family face and saw only faces no kin could recognize.

I wished I was still up a burning tree in the Wilderness, my general dead, my own life limited to minutes more.

They took me out the south gate the next morning into Captain Wirz's headquarters.

"What do you have to say for yourself?"

"Well, I'm not really a Yankee, I'm only a fifteen-year-old mountain boy from East Tennessee down here looking for my daddy and my brothers, and I stripped a dead Yankee of his uniform so's I could move more freely among the Yankees."

He looked into my eyes, and I reckon he knew they had seen the War. My height told on me and what the years and weather and battle had done to my face showed me up for a liar. Still, in about a month, I would turn fifteen.

"I believe you are not a Yankee," he said, "but I am convinced that you are a Rebel deserter in a Yankee uniform. Take him out and shoot him."

They took me over to the dead house and they stood me up against a wall.

But before they could get lined up to shoot at me, a work detail of Yankee prisoners came in, and one of them yelled, "Hello, Sharpshooter, what they about to do to you?"

And I said, "Well, now where did I know you?"

He said, "Don't you remember that time we met in the middle of the Tennessee River with tobacco and playing cards to exchange in our mouths, water twenty feet deep, freezing cold, dog-paddling?"

Shivering now in the June sun and about to cry and about to piss in my pants, I appreciated him giving me that sharp moment to remember during the rest of my short life.

"We knew you for one of the best Sharpshooters in Longstreet's whole army!"

And so they marched him on inside the prison.

As the firing squad was setting up to do what I had witnessed so many times for desertion or murder or rape or even in some places petty theft, I remembered the sound of voices in a blackberry thicket on the lower slopes of our Mountain under a 2 o'clock sun.

The Rebel captain who was getting the men lined up straight to shoot me, turned to me, said, "Is he telling the truth, are you a Sharpshooter?"

And I bragged, yes, I was with General Longstreet and named all the battles I could recall, ending with the Wilderness, and said I had started home because Old Pete was dead, and the officer said, no, the latest word was that he was only badly wounded and couldn't speak, and I came alive and smiled, and then he said, "Let's see you prove it," and so he took a rifle off a man in the firing squad, and it was a sorry contraption, but I asked for three tries on a target that he said nobody could hit.

And the thousands inside the walls who heard but didn't see must have wondered what kind of lowlife trash they had just shot that caused the firing squad to cheer its own work.

So I went up into one of the guard towers, some meager rations in one hand, a half-decent rifle in the other, only twenty minutes later, with Captain Wirz's blessing, because they told me they had two problems: Lee needed experienced men so badly in Virginia, the stockade was forced to use Georgia militia, which was mostly boys as young as ten and men as old as seventy-five, who thought that any Yankee who so much as sneezed within a foot of the deadline, even though some had built one end of their tents and shebangs right up on the deadline rail, was a signal for a mass insurrection, and they would fire away, convinced that killing a Yankee would make them famous throughout the Confederacy by the next morning. At night, they were more jittery than by day. "What is called for is discipline," the officer told me, "an animal none of these fellows has ever seen." And there I was, come back from the living dead to help out. I felt as if I was on a furlough from death.

The other problem was related to the first: there were a great many dead earnest escape attempts.

"This is a prime spot," Captain Wirz told me in his German accent. "You fail to shoot or you miss, you will become a deserter again."

That probably gave me sharp eyesight, but I remember less about that year at Andersonville than anywhere else.

Seems like I remember that when one man tried to escape, compassion made me misfire. But he must not have got away or I would be no more.

Every day I looked into the faces below for the face of at least one of my kin, all I could ever hope to see, maybe even Tim, but saw none.

Sometimes, especially in the night, it was sort of like the camplife that had always been the part of the war when I felt most alive and would remember most clearly.

Most of the time, you understand, that prison was nothing like camplife, more like hell's mimicry of camplife. And the Andersonville Raiders made it a greater hell than it might otherwise have been. The raiders were prisoners who robbed the weak and sick and wounded and who beat and killed those who refused to obey. Captain Wirz let the victims set up their own system of justice and they were given lumber to construct a gallows where they hanged six of the leaders and Wirz left the gallows as a reminder, until the prisoners, foot by foot, dismantled it to keep warm one more night or to build shelters.

❧ ❧ ❧

One day I looked down and this Negro was leaning up against the deadline post, playing, looked to me, like he was reading a newspaper! A newspaper! Brazen as all hell. Well, now that made me mad. Teasing a poor ignorant mountain boy by pretending to read that newspaper in front of me, knowing I couldn't read myself. Greatgrandfather was the only one who could, and he was too mean to teach anybody else. So I could neither read *nor* write.

I yelled down, "You asking for it!"

"What?"

I said, "Acting like you reading that thing."

"Now! I *can* read," he said, "and I'll teach *you* how, if you want me to."

What he was reading was Cherokee writing that he told me was made up out of nothing by an Indian named Sequoyah of the Cherokee nation from just west of Knoxville. The only man in recorded history who ever made up a whole new set of letters. And he had done it to free his people from the power of the white man's language.

This Negro Yankee soldier had been a slave to a Cherokee Indian plantation owner, and his master taught him how to read and used him as a translator between his family and the white man. And when the War started, his master went into the Rebel army and took him with him to translate, and they got captured, and this Negro was forced into the Yankee army, and that's how he ended up in Andersonville Prison, with me guarding over him from that tower.

He told me that story about Sequoyah making up that new set of letters and I loved to hear it more than once. It got me to where I wanted to read and write Cherokee, and so he taught me how to read and write it.

I have tried hard, especially when I am out hunting, to get more of that time in the guard tower at Andersonville in my sights, so to say, but I can't do it.

A Survivor of the Sinking of the *Sultana*

WHEN WORD REACHED US OF LEE'S SURRENDER AT APPOMATTOX, WE broke up Andersonville.

After the guards and their prisoners had been released from prison, I slipped away from that place where I had watched many of the 12,000 out of the 45,000 die.

Most went to surrender, but I soon took up with some officers who said President Davis had been captured and who were heading West to set up a Trans-Mississippi Confederacy, although for my own part, I just had an inclination to roam out there in the West.

But near Vicksburg, I heard that 2,000 survivors of Andersonville, Cahaba, and other Confederate prisons had been assembled at Vicksburg for transport north to be mustered out of the Union army. When I learned that about 400 of them were East Tennessee Unionists, I lagged behind General Smith's fugitives and got me some civilian clothes and went to Vicksburg to see if I could find my grandpa, my daddy, or my brothers among the freed prisoners. Tim, too, because I always felt guilty imagining he was among the hanged at Lick Creek Bridge.

I found the Mississippi out of its banks, levees overflowed, and the river full of flood debris. Snows thawing in Canada and Minnesota had swollen the river and the water I dashed on my face was freezing cold.

Three steamboats were tied up at the piers, but a Negro dock hand told me that all the soldiers were going to be loaded onto the *Sultana*, which had already taken on about 100 men, women, and children passengers in New Orleans. So I paid more than I was worth to get on among them, and almost immediately I heard an officer of the boat ask a man who was loading horses and mules, "Did you hear that the president has been assassinated?"

"Oh, yes! Oh, yes!" the man said, and I sensed he was a local man who kept back his tears for somebody closer to his heart.

As I waited, I heard a constant, nerve-wracking clanging from the boiler where men were doing repairs.

"I thought those old tubular type of boilers had been done away with before this," one of the workers said to another as they stopped to smoke.

As the soldiers came aboard, I watched for my people, as I had at Andersonville, but I didn't have a very good vantage point, and I already knew and saw again in the faces of the men coming aboard that it takes only a few months in a prison like Andersonville to change a man's face, even his body, forever. And they came on in such swarms, I wasn't surprised to be told that this boat would normally carry no more than 500. They were loaded and packed in the same way the cargo of hogs were packed, maybe worse. Many were sick and weak and thin as wagon spokes.

"Buck up, comrade," one soldier said, to the sick one he was helping up the gangplank, "it's home-sweet-home for you now."

"I don't care anymore," his comrade said.

But most of them, sick and dying or not, were talking and singing of nothing but home-sweet-home.

One man said to his comrade, "I've just had a good look at that boiler they're repairing. We had better get off this boat and make it on our own to Camp Chase."

But I saw them later making a place for themselves at the head of the stairway.

By the time the *Sultana* started upriver, I had not found any of my kin.

The next day at Helena, Arkansas, we discharged some cargo and took on something else, I don't know what, because I was paying attention to a photographer on the bank who was taking a picture of the *Sultana* in its new role as troop transport. Some of the men rushed to the rail to get in the picture, and I hoped he would finish before many more squeezed up to the rail because I felt, or imagined I felt, the boat complain and list.

I kept hearing Andersonville Prison more often than any other, so I kept my head down, spoke to no one, tried to act like one of the civilians. When I recognized two men who had escaped last winter from the prison hospital, I kept even more to the shadows.

At Memphis where about a hundred hogsheads of sugar were being unloaded, I went ashore, half intending to stay there, because I had neither seen nor heard about any of my kin. But I reckoned that maybe I would find them at Camp Chase where many others were being mustered out, and it would be grand for us all—or we who had survived—to go home together and surprise my Greatgrandfather and my mother and my grandmother and my younger brothers and sisters who I was supposed to have been watching over all this time. So at midnight when they got ready to go again, I stepped onto the gangplank.

We crossed the river to take on a load of coal and then churned north toward our destination, Cairo, Illinois, where the men were to board the train to Camp Chase.

Shuddering in the cold breeze that swept the decks, I, despite my fears, took a look at the area around the boiler. Too many crowded around it for anyone else to get within a hundred feet. I looked longingly at a spot in front of the pilot house. Finally, I lay myself down on the hurricane deck, forward of the wheelhouse.

At about 3 A.M., eight miles above Memphis, April 27, 1865, an explosion woke 2,000 ex-prisoners of war and about 100 men, women, and children passengers—no, of the over 1,500 who perished, many did not awaken, but were launched into Eternity in innocent sleep.

At this moment, my chest remembers the stick of firewood that struck me.

I was certain General Nathan Bedford Forrest's "gunboat cavalry" had fired upon us—just as several men had predicted he would. We were a prize catch for a commander who always seized opportunities that offered the least danger to his own men.

Staggering on the hurricane deck among men who jostled me at every turn, I worked over to the rail and below me saw men running out of a smothering cloud of steam, scalded, some falling dead, some hurling themselves, pushing others with them, into the dark water. It was not General Forrest this time, but the boat's boiler that had exploded.

Crazed men walked the deck wringing their hands. Women and children and the old and feeble ran about, screaming. A man lay crushed under a huge chunk of the boat's bell.

Struggling along the rail in search of a place from which to dive into the water, the deck on fire behind me, I looked down into a gigantic hole full of blue flames and watched men slide on the slanting deck into it.

Weak and faint and suffocating from the smoke and steam, I saw Greatgrandfather sitting by "the place of fire," beckoning to me, and saw myself running with the ease of a child toward him, but I heard Brownlow's bellowing voice, "Let the names be given!" and I thought, "Yes, a voice forged in hell," as the man in the Knoxville prison had said. "Not *my* name!" I screamed, making a rush for the deck of the wheelhouse, mindful of the wounded man in front of me intent on the same escape. Suddenly, he disappeared, and I caught hold of something at the edge of the deck to hold back from falling, and looked down, and there was the wounded man, between the deck and the wheelhouse which had broken loose from the boat, and he was caught, as in a vise, between, half in water, half in fire, screaming.

Others jumped on top of the wheelhouse and were clinging to it when it broke loose entirely and sunk, in a hissing cloud of steam, into the river.

"She's sinking!" men screamed now.

I picked up a plank and found a place at the rail for jumping. Stripped for swimming, I looked out over the water, black with men, who were grabbing objects or grabbing onto each other. Poised to drop, I glimpsed a man pinned under a cow in grotesque embrace on the main deck below, then let go.

I came up strangling, feeling that all the world was only my lungs and the river that was invading them.

As I pulled at my plank, men pulled at *me,* and not all of them were unable to swim, but all were in panic.

I saw some skiffs and a picket boat, rescuing people, and soldiers lined the shore ready to help. But I was mid-river, too far.

Men clung to staging planks and flood-wood and to bales of hay, and to barrels that slipped, rolling mockingly, from their lunging grasp. Some prayed, some swore, some were crying, some were singing, and a few did all that in rapid sequence even as I floated past them.

One man yelled over to me, asking did I have a chew of tobacco I would swap for his shoes, so droll I felt maybe he needed irony more than his shoes, which were ten pounds of water-logged leather that even as I watched pulled him down to perdition.

It was worse than any battle I was ever in, worse than Andersonville, because it was all the battles and prisons packed into a single explosion and sinking.

A cramp caught hold of me, sudden as clapping your hands together. I let loose of my staging plank and, in that moment when I was certain I was to drown, I felt—as if it started inside my chest and was beating to get out—the cold, northern snow thawing.

But flood-wood struck me and I clung to it and let the current carry me toward the Arkansas shore.

I saw an alligator the flood had washed into the river. Each piece of wood became an alligator.

I saw a sleeping man up in a cottonwood tree, lashed to it with cloth that I took to be his own shirt.

I got caught near shore in the branches of a fallen tree that had hit a snag. A swarm of buffalo gnats had set upon me when I saw some home-bound Confederate soldiers wading out to me, their arms spread for balance. Are they going to arrest me again, for desertion, I wondered. No, all compassion, they delivered me from the river and the buffalo gnats.

In their arms, freezing naked, I looked back between their shoulders at the burning wreck. Not to be counted among the 1,500 souls that had perished, I had survived, more dead than alive.

After a few days among the living, I set out to catch up with General Kirby Smith who was looking for a place to set up a new nation.

We reached Palmetto near the border with Mexico the Sunday after the battle there, the last battle of the war—a Confederate victory, as was the first battle, at Sumter, which I also missed.

I had heard by then about the Mexican-American War that ended in 1848, the year I was born. And, I figured out years later, I had sort of followed Sequoyah's route when he wandered in search of a legendary Indian

Eden and was buried in a grave unknown. Now as I write, I vaguely remember thinking of him there in Palmetto.

I wandered, drifted, took up with women, mostly older than I was, and to make a living, I sketched, in Texas saloons for a drink—sometimes from a photograph. When they insisted that I sign my name, I would do it in Cherokee and once or twice it made a man want to fight. It was one hell-raising tear across the West that lasted two years, and I wound up with a dead man at my feet in a saloon in a town too new to have a name. Brawl. Say the word, low or loud, and you *feel* what it is, you almost have the whole thing there in your mouth—got to spit it out.

Going Home

From the Cupola of Vicksburg Courthouse

BECAUSE I HAD LET IT SLIP THAT I WAS A SURVIVOR OF THE SINKING OF the *Sultana,* the editor of the Elizabethton newspaper kept after me for years, when I would go to him with skins or wild berries to sell, to tell my story. "You need to tell your story, Willis," he kept saying.

I kept telling him, no, I didn't need to tell nothing. Nor did I feel anybody needed to read my story.

After listening to so many people talk about the war, I told him the whole story in 1876, and he wrote it down for me, and then I took a while to add things to it, and cut the cussing. I don't to this day know why I finally gave in.

As I read my brief chapters over again, knowing they would appear in the newspaper each week, I knew I had been right. No need at all—not for me, not for anybody, especially Reverend Carter—to hear my story. It sounded like a confession I wasn't ready yet to make. So I told him, no, he couldn't publish it.

But in the years since, it has not been over for me. It keeps coming back.

But what seems now more important, as I look back, is not this happened and then this happened and sure enough something else and something else happened, but how everything happened all over again in different ways in my own head and imagination years after the war was over. You would think that once it was over, certainly a decade gone, the thing would be still, so a body could look at it, but after all these years, it is like a nest of cottonmouths.

I have rewritten now what my editor friend wrote down, and put the cussing back in. I've kept the rest of the story—about coming home and being home—under my hat all these years now. I don't know yet why I want to set that down, too, this part that I am writing now, but I do.

Now, I am picking up where I left off two decades ago.

I stayed out in the West, wandering, on a two-year drunk, scratching a living in saloons by drawing folks' faces to send back east. I had the knack for drawing. People would say, "Draw my picture," and I'd draw their picture for another drink, and I made it to my eighteenth birthday that way, just drawing and drinking and brawling. And I got enough of it. I said, "Willis Carr, it's time you went home," to Carter County, up on Holston Mountain.

So two years after the war was over, I struck out for the Mountain.

Leading my foot-sore horse along the trail from Shreveport, I let the white cupola, tall and graceful as the church spire to the north of it, draw me toward the town, though I was drifting east anyway.

Crossing the Mississippi River on the ferry, I had to hold myself in to keep from falling into a panic, feeling it all keenly again, that night when we all exploded off the *Sultana,* maybe my kin, too, that night in the river when most of us drowned.

I watched the courthouse grow larger, even more commanding on the skyline. From under the bluff, I saw now only the cupola, but the white columns are as clear in my mind as the sky. I climb the steep hill in the mud that last night's thunderstorm has left, surprised at the sight of caves honeycombing the banks on each side, made by the deep cut of the street in the face of the cliff.

What I had thought was the front of the white building, presenting shadowed columns to the West, overlooking the river, is duplicated east, north, south—four equally important entrances. I discover that it is the courthouse of Warren County that I have entered.

From the round cupola, open to a faint breeze off the Mississippi, drenched in sweat, my heart pumping at a brisk canter, I look out over Vicksburg, north and south, then northwest again, seeing the river make a great horse shoe bend, the village of Desoto on the peninsula, then look due west over Louisiana toward Shreveport from which I had ridden, then look north again, see the river coming down to the bend and a smaller river coming down from the east, and up there, a cemetery on the bluffs overlooking the river, and then my gaze returns northeast, seeing another cemetery a mile from the town, then a white house on the main road in the direction I will soon go myself. I see rugged bluffs, and cannon, and muddy roads, and paths that climb and descend and wind over the roughest terrain I had seen since I rode out of East Texas, terrain torn by gullies and ravines entangled in vines, with open spaces under the bright blue sky that look at first like more cemeteries, but that I finally see are cotton patches in bloom. Cut by seven red clay roads, two narrow bayous, and a railroad track, this maze of vines, mud, hills, and ravines east of the courthouse fans out from north to south along the river. South of the town, across the river, a canal cuts, incomplete, into the peninsula.

Cooled and calmed, I go down to satisfy my desire to walk that mangled terrain.

Mud on the narrow, twisting roads and paths pulls at my high western boots, wears me down, giving me a terrifying sense of walking, a ghost, on the bottom of the Mississippi River. When I approach an enormous crater, overgrown with briars, vines, and saplings, I rush away from it, wanting distance and height on it. I fight dense undergrowth, eating a few blackberries and wild grapes as I struggle to get up out of a ravine that I suspect is full of rattlesnakes. I climb a treeless slope that will give me a higher vantage point on the crater, discover that the depth of the crater is now lost to my field of vision. I am a survivor again. But the afterimage of it is still so clear, I open my sketch pad and, as if I am a hovering raven, look down on the crater, and begin to draw, feeling that I am the only soul within miles.

Drawing a Yankee at the Crater on the Battlefield

BUT I WAS NOT ALONE. A MAN'S HEAD SHOWED JUST ABOVE THE FARTHER rim of the crater, as if he were just now surfacing, another survivor of the *Sultana*. I felt an impulse to reach for my rifle, get him in my telescopic sights, and blow his brains out. It came to me that I had seldom been any angrier at all the other targets than I was at this man, and that I still, despite two years of drunkenness, could plug a third eye beneath his brows. He climbed on up and stood there on the rim, on one leg, on crutches. Then he started down, coming *toward* but not *to* me. He was wandering, gazing around, stopping to stare at the ground. Then I lost him. He is not going to make it, one-legged, through that ravine, that morass of vigorous vegetation, if that's what he has set out to do.

But by the time I had completed the sketch, he was shifting to get a look over my shoulder.

"You got the gift." I didn't know enough then about the skill of sketching to contradict him.

I told him I thought the terrain here looked strange, and he said in a

Yankee accent that the siege had torn it all up, and when I asked, "What siege?" he stepped back so abruptly he almost lost his prop and fell back down the slope.

"Why, the siege of Vicksburg in '63."

And I said, "Oh, yes, I remember hearing about it."

And he said, "Where was *you?*"

And I said, "Oh, out West. I look old for my age." I was only eighteen that July.

He wasn't interested in me after that, but just like a Yankee, he came right out and said it: "Draw my picture." Usually, it took me two hours to work a man into position to make me an offer, but this one was vain from the start. "If I was to get over there on the rim of the crater, would you draw me into your picture and sell it to me?"

They would say, "Draw my portrait. Or draw my wife from this photograph." But never, "Draw me into a landscape"—especially one I had already rendered. But the word "sell" triggered "Sure."

I told him he didn't have to climb back down into that ravine. "I can look at you standing here, sir, and just stick you in it."

"No, it must be authentic," he said, a little offended. Making a snug fit for his crutches in his armpits, he shoved off. "Just give me a little time."

Having plenty of time, I gave him some of it.

Just as I lost him again, his voice rose to me on heat waves. "Can you put a uniform on me if I describe it to you?"

And I said, "No need to describe it, I saw some out West."

I knew that this moment meant more to him than such moments had meant to any of the men whose faces I had drawn from Georgia to Mexico and back.

In an hour, he was back up on the rim, but only a one-legged silhouette against the sun. When he yelled to me, it made me remember the way we answered the Yankee voices at night, or during a truce for burial details.

"I would sure appreciate it, if you would add a leg!"

I started to ask, "Whose leg?" but he was in a mood that his eyes had sort of cast over *me*. And I needed the money.

So I draw him in, so that he's wearing the uniform and standing on *two* legs, and without trying, I magnify his face in my imagination until I see his eyes again, giving me that look from deep inside himself, and I keep seeing the cross-hairs of the telescopic sight, and then, maybe it is the sun beating down on me, but I am inside his eyes, looking back out over the ravine into my own eyes.

I waved the drawing above my head. From the moment he started back down into the ravine, I knew he already had it clearly in his head, that he had imagined it as I sketched him in, and saw himself now in a special way that would be important until the day he died.

That was when I asked myself, "Why doesn't it mean that much to me? The War. Or any particular moment of it?" I started to yell across the ravine to him that I really had been in it. For four years. Starting when I was thirteen. But he was yelling over to me, "Meet me on the Jackson Road at The White House."

As I walked in the direction he had pointed out, the image that the phrase "The White House" conjured was so familiar, I felt I would recognize the house when I got there.

As I came around a bend, the house was there on a rise. There were big gouges in the side of the hill, as if a great many Parrot guns had missed the white target a great many times. The house needed some repair, but not from bombardment damage.

Stumbling up the hill, I sat on the porch to wait for him. When he came and sat beside me, he took the drawing and stared a long time at himself standing on the rim of the crater.

He told me The White House was the only house still standing on the battlefield, that it was a mystery the Confederates never destroyed it.

"Which side was you on?"

I said, "It's over. There isn't any side."

Looking at the drawing again, the veteran said, "I'm glad to hear you say that."

I tell him that when I heard of the siege of Vicksburg, I always imagined the fighting in the streets of the town itself, as in one town whose name I couldn't then recall, the Yankees firing across the river into the town and then crossing on pontoon bridges to get at the Confederates who waited behind a long stone wall.

He said, no, it wasn't like Mayre's Heights at Fredericksburg, more like Antietam or Gettysburg, fighting outside the town, or more like Petersburg, where there was a siege, too, and also a crater.

"I see they've tore down Coonskin's Tower."

"Said what?"

"Coonskin's Tower. Confederate Sharpshooters gave us such hell that Second Lieutenant Henry C. Foster, Company B, 23rd Indiana took the rails and ties from the Jackson railroad we tore up after the battle of Big Black River Bridge and worked nights to build himself a tower so high he could look right down into their works." The one-legged veteran didn't take his eyes off the drawing of himself in the landscape. "He let them know what a Sharpshooter really was. Wore a raccoon cap up there. Like to get whoever tore it down in *my* sights."

I imagined plain enough how the terrain would look from up there.

"They tell me they didn't celebrate the Fourth of July here this year nor last," he said, as if for obvious reasons, making me curious.

"Why not?"

And he said, "Don't you know that's the day Pemberton surrendered to General Grant?"

"I was out West myself." A lie was better than saying I had forgot.

"The very day after the battle of Gettysburg."

So while "Coonskin" was up in his tower there, trying to pick off Confederate officers or artillerymen, a Confederate Sharpshooter in Devil's Den was trying to get one of "Coonskin's" brother officers on Little Round Top in his own sights.

The veteran seemed to notice how agitated I was. Well, he was agitated, too, but deeper down inside himself than I was.

"Ain't you gonna ask me how I lost my leg?"

"I didn't think a body ought to."

"In the crater. We used saprollers to protect us while we dug a tunnel under their redan—the Third Louisiana's—and blew it up, but they were on to us, and they'd pulled back a little. I helped dig alongside about thirty men who'd been coal miners before the war, and I was in the van that rushed in after the explosion, expecting close fighting. The explosion threw up a high mound of dirt, and they were behind it, and they lobbed fuse-timed shells over to us, and so that's how I came to leave a leg here somewhere when I went home to Cincinnati. I just wanted to see the *place*." It struck me as odd that it was my drawing he stared at as he talked.

He got up and said he would show me, on the way back to town, where everything happened. I wasn't eager for a tour, but I didn't want to hurt his feelings, and he hadn't paid me yet.

He told me that men had dug caves, bombproofs all around this side
of the house, that it was somewhere here around this very house that surgeons with glistening bloodstains up to their elbows had hacked off his leg
and tossed it up on a pile of limbs.

We walked down the path a piece, and I noticed a rough shaft of stone
a little below us, and he said, "Let's rest." We did, and he said, "Here's
the very spot where General Grant and Pemberton met to talk over the
surrender, under a scrawny oak tree that our men cut to pieces for souve-
nirs, and I see others have come along and notched this monument, too."

I wanted to tell him that I didn't understand any of that. I wanted to
confess that I had been a Confederate Sharpshooter with General Longstreet in most of his battles, but I didn't want to introduce to him a different
person just when he was acting like he had got me fixed in his mind as a
young man of the West who was wandering back into history.

As we walked on, he showed me a cave that a Confederate officer's ser-
vant had dug for his wife, so she could be near him, and told me that many
citizens of the Gibraltar of the Americas, as he relished calling Vicksburg—
just as he called the river "The Father of Waters," with capitals in his
voice—had dug caves and lived in them along the cliff to escape the bombardment. "Most of the caves in town are sealed up again, but this one's
been left alone."

And I'm going to sleep there tonight, I told myself, because even with
what he paid me, I wouldn't have enough to squander on a room in the
Washington Hotel he directed me to.

"The caves haunt me," he said, as we reached a street on the outskirts
of the town, within sight of the courthouse cupola. "I could have been
buried in one at The White House." He told about "Whistlin' Dick," a
Confederate cannon that still disturbs his sleep. "An old slave got buried
alive in one of these caves. They tried to dig him out—he was property to
save, don't you know—but he denied them and stayed buried." Maybe
he was one of the slaves who built the courthouse two years before the war,
as I heard one man telling another when I came down from the cupola.
"Another nigger named Graham was helping the Rebels dig a countermine," said the veteran, as if desperate for us to part laughing. "There
was an accident, and he got blowed sky-high all the way over behind our
lines, and lived to joke about it, and be famous for a week or so."

"I Am the Man Who Shot General Sanders!"

NORTHEAST OF VICKSBURG, I GOT ON THE OLD NATCHEZ TRACE AND LET it take me where it was going. I wasn't in any hurry. I wanted to see my Greatgrandfather. And to see my mother and my daddy and grandpa and my older brothers and my little brothers and sisters and whoever of my kin had survived, from the burning of the bridges to the sinking of the *Sultana*. But unlike all other men I'd met, I wasn't sick with longing for home. I felt a half-hearted pull toward South Holston Mountain. I wanted to *drift* home.

I thought the one-legged Yankee veteran's astonishing nostalgia for the War was uncommon until I got into Tennessee around Franklin on the Harpeth River (I had by-passed Shiloh) where people talked about the ten Confederate generals killed, wounded, or missing on the November afternoon when General Hood and General Forrest went after Schofield and Sheridan. "Boys this will be quick but desperate," several men quoted a Confederate office. Ten thousand men died with the generals, they told me. "One of Forrest's cavalrymen fell off his horse—his head on one side, his body on the other."

When I walked over the battle area around Carter House, I didn't find any lost soul looking for his leg, Yankee or Rebel, and I was painful hungry and without a customer. But I could tell that for most people, it wasn't really over. Not because you couldn't walk anywhere without tripping over a Yankee soldier or carpetbagger speculator in cotton, or a freed slave unwilling to contract to Southerners, but something in the air that came out in windbag loafers who couldn't talk about anything without the War being in it somewhere. "Why, to get to Nashville from Franklin, you have to cross that bridge the Yankees built, or if you're like me, you'd rather swim across Harpeth." I rode across the bridge.

When I cut over to Murfreesboro and found out General Bragg and Rosecrans lost twenty-six thousand men between them on Stone's River just below the town, it was the same thing. I walked around the Widow Smith's house where most of them were killed, and all a man wanted to tell me, three times and more, was how when the firing started, he never saw such a sight of rabbits running out of the woods ahead of "our boys." Well, that was *it* for him, I reckon.

And all around Nashville, I ran into men of both sides who had fought there, as if two years ago was yesterday. "It was awful around Granny White's House. This young girl come running out in the road a-cryin' and begged General Hood to quit, and when Thomas finally forced him to retreat, some private stumbled into his tent by mistake, and there sat General Hood a-cryin'."

I did find several that paid me to draw them in front of the capitol building on the hill, posing stiff in front of white columns. I heard some talk about Governor Brownlow, but at that time, I did not make the connection to Greatgrandfather's Parson Brownlow.

The one-legged Yankee haunted me the whole time, and I began to feel as if *I* was missing some part of myself.

Drifting east up the Great Valley of Tennessee, I began to seek out men who wanted to talk about the War, at first only as customers to get enough food in my belly to keep going, but after a while, I was drawn to them out of bewilderment. They remembered everything. All I could remember was camp, though in no particular place. The thousand places seemed to be the same place, always in the woods, and by the time I had pulled back and followed them, the firestarter, the waterfinder, and the cook, who always seemed to rise up out of the ranks when and where they were needed, had already done their work, and the storyteller was at it, or maybe the singing had already begun, and as one of the Sharpshooters who helped make it possible for them to camp with some hope of peace, I was welcome to share the fire, the water, maybe even some of the scarce coffee to wash down my hardtack. And I remembered the times I saw General Longstreet.

But most men drawled out the names of places and battles and the dates with no effort at recollection, and I didn't have them to tell. Most of them were gray-bearded men who made me feel they had fought in a different War from the one I had forgotten, because, although I was among the very youngest, and certainly the youngest *Sharpshooter* I knew about, they had *all* been young two years before. Like Rip Van Winkle, I thought these veterans were playing tricks on me.

In Pulaski (birthplace, I learned later, of the Ku Kluxers), I was drawing a man, putting a uniform on him, an idea I offered that struck him as real bright and that upped the charge to a silver dollar, when a bystander piped in with, "The feller's picture you *ought* to draw is this one here."

"Why?"

"Well, he's the man who shot—"

"Don't you start that! That's *private*."

"Private, hell, you told everybody that comes through this town, you told *us* thirty times, can't you tell him once't?"

I looked at the graybearded man who sat in a rocker, back against the hotel wall. He leaned over, spit slowly, just missing the toe of his own shoe, and looked off down the street as if his friend hadn't pointed him out to me.

"I wonder if I could draw him to where you could tell just by looking at it, he's the man who shot—whoever it was?"

"Hear that, Tom? Give him a dollar to see if he can."

"I told you fellers, it's a secret just amongst ourselves."

"Secret, hell, I never heard such braggin' from a human."

"Well, wouldn't *you*, if it'd been you? Instead of one long furlough in Elmira Prison?"

I started sketching him.

"I ain't gonna pay for it."

"You don't *have* to pay for it," I said, working his eyes, "'less you like it."

As I sketched him, he talked and ended up telling it.

"Well, what these boys talking about, what made *me* famous in the War was that I'm the one that shot General Sanders."

I didn't know who General Sanders was. I didn't know what he was talking about. I asked, "Where?"

He said, "At Knoxville."

So I says, "I think I was *in* Knoxville." My brain was so scattered from drinking, and I was too young to remember everything anyway. "I think I was *in* Knoxville."

"Big old house they got down there called Bleak House, I got up in the tower," Tom said, holding still without me telling him. "He rode a white horse, coming down the Kingston Pike west of Knoxville, and I was up in the tower of Bleak House with four other Sharpshooters, but they was all dead around me—when I saw General Sanders riding toward the house on the road below, out in front of his men, like he was scouting on his own. I got him in my sights and he was a dead man. Only general of Southern birth killed while serving in the damned Union army. They named the fort after him, and I was in the attack on it. Sunday, November 29, 1863, by God. I killed him, I'm the one, very one you're drawing a picture of."

I believed him, because I didn't remember a damned thing. Who would remember a fever dream?

I began then to become more conscious of what happens to a man when you sketch him. By the time you finish, he's a different person. I reckon that's why nobody ever looks like the drawing of him. Tom told it again, filling in more detail, sheets of ice on the berme, telegraph wire stretched along the ground, blood ankle-deep in the ditch, getting younger under his gray hairs, and told it a third time with even more facts and embellishments, like most men do, answering questions, until I passed my drawing over to him.

"What you want to make a thirty-year-old man look like Methuslah for?"

"You don't have to pay."

But he wasn't reluctant to pay because, he said, he ought to pass something down to his grandchildren, and I wanted to tell him that I, too, was in the attack on Fort Sanders, but his story had only just now reminded me, I had not clearly remembered it for a long time, and his telling it had made it come back in vivid images like a blast from a shotgun. So I wasn't ready to tell much of anything, and I knew if they asked questions, I'd feel foolish not knowing what to say, so I kept mum.

Return to "The Place of Fire"

As I drifted on, now more directly toward Holston Mountain, September now, wanting to get home before the cold set in, that Rebel veteran perched on the gallery in front of the hotel at Pulaski competed with the lunging one-legged Yankee as a figure, a voice, that kept coming back in the flesh or in my memory of them as I had drawn them, and also as I drew them again and again, differently, in different poses and places, in my mind, for I seldom drew just for my own amusement.

Because I didn't feel the way they did, didn't remember much, I worried that maybe something was wrong with me, or that I was not like other men, somehow. I never told any of the men I met that I had been with General Longstreet at Sharpsburg, Gettysburg, Chickamauga, Lookout Mountain, Knoxville, and the Wilderness, and many other places that I couldn't remember a name for. Nobody mentioned the sinking of the *Sultana,* and so to have survived seemed of no importance to anyone but me.

I began to be aware again of Rebel and Yankee, North and South, and since I had shifted from one side to the other several times and since it was now a time of terrible turmoil and I finally heard that it was Parson Brownlow who was Reconstruction Governor, I was unable to declare myself to others and so realized that I was unable to declare myself to myself either. When men asked *me* questions about the War, I had to answer "no" mostly.

I just went on, I met a lot of other people, I heard a lot of other people talking this and that about the Civil War, and I was wondering, "Well, you know, I was there, but I don't remember all *this,* and why are these people so . . . ? Why do they talk about it all the time, why do they want to sit around talking about it, what *is* it about it? That was just something I did, then I went out West."

I began to feel that where I was wandering was one vast battlefield that was vanishing under weeds and saplings right before my eyes.

South Holston Mountain drew me slowly back.

Going through Knoxville, I didn't even stop to look around.

During the war, campfires made me homesick or made me feel right at home because to me home was my Greatgrandfather sitting by the fireplace, reading or meditating or declaring and declaiming. When I walked in the door, the cabin looked abandoned, and he was of course dead, sitting there by the fireplace, dead. The cabin had been abandoned.

And I thought, "Well, that's the way he'd want to go."

He had written in ash on the mantle: DO NOT TOUCH ME. LET ME TURN TO DUST, THEN SWEEP ME OUT THE FRONT DOOR. BECAUSE THIS IS ME, AND I AM IN MY PLACE. By the fireplace. "The place of fire," as I called it when I was little. That was the picture I had carried throughout the war and the two-year drunk and brawl out West.

I dug his grave. When I went to pick him up, still sitting in his chair, the heft was so sudden—for I expected more weight, as if he were still the heavy presence I had known as a child and I were still that child—he fell apart and scattered over the floor. Somehow that aggravated the fool out of me and, with something short of reverence, I swept him right into "the place of fire."

Coming back after six years, I felt the cabin was a stranger.

I returned to doing what I had learned, just before the War, to do well, and what I continue to do to this day. I hunted. And I traded the skins, and I got by.

After a few weeks, I went down the Mountain to Elizabethton and visited my mother and little brothers and sisters.

"And where have *you* been all these years?" my mother asked me, in a tone of voice that told me it hadn't crossed her mind that I had fought in the War. I was about to tell her I had fought for the Confederacy, as her side of the family had, but she said, "Your father and your brothers—they hanged Tim at Lick Creek Bridge—and your grandpa were all killed or died in prison camps. When they brought me the news that your daddy drowned in the Mississippi River with fifteen hundred other souls, I come back down the Mountain to Elizabethton and my people. I have married a widower with six children for me to raise. I have a new life, Willis."

I could tell by her voice she was going to forget as much as she could. So I put off telling that I had survived the *Sultana* explosion, even that I had fought on the Confederate side. "Oh, wandering out West," was all I said, and I saw the West in her eyes as something everybody imagines as a vast, fabled place to go when you want to get away and start over, as she was doing right there in the town where she was born.

I saw her and my brothers and sisters almost every time I went down into Elizabethton for rations and supplies, but everything had changed, I came back to no continuity. And I never did tell my mother I fought with the Confederacy and survived the *Sultana*. Nobody knew any of that until years later, when I finally told my editor friend, and now you.

Reverend Carter Teaches Me
How to Read and Write

MY GREATGRANDFATHER COULD READ AND WRITE VERY WELL, BUT HE HAD not got around to teaching me, so I had gone out into the world unable. When I was an unwilling guard at Andersonville Prison the last year of the War, a Yankee soldier who was a black slave of the Cherokee taught me how to read and write Sequoyah's Cherokee syllabary to pass the time. When I returned to the cabin on the Mountain, I was still unable to read or write English.

Most of the world's great names and faces were zero to me then. The only books I saw were the Bible and cheap editions of Bunyan's *Pilgrim's Progress* and Milton's *Paradise Lost,* but only Greatgrandfather could read, so that the only notable men I ever heard about were those that happened to turn up mentioned, praised, or attacked, in Parson Brownlow's Knoxville *Whig* as Greatgrandfather read it aloud. Its full name was *Brownlow's Knoxville Whig & Rebel Ventilator,* as if announcing the long title of visiting royalty. A book's fine print goes to the brain, but Brownlow's newspaper sentences were like buckshot to the body.

As a way of conjuring the presence of my Greatgrandfather, I sat by the fire and stared at the pages of print and illustrations of what I later learned was Milton's *Paradise Lost*, Shakespeare's complete plays, John Bunyan's *Pilgrim's Progress,* and a pristine copy of the book known to thousands of readers, mostly in the North, as *Parson Brownlow's Book,* from a journal kept in the prison where I had seen him and where he had read passages to us—tales of atrocities and his persecution and how they had "vomited me" out of the Confederacy—and Greatgrandfather had left behind a complete file of *Whigs*—what Brownlow's rival editor of the Knoxville *Register* called "that tower of Babel"—from Brownlow's early newspaper days, starting in Elizabethton, as a matter of fact, on up to that "burn the bridges" editorial out of Knoxville. As I looked through them, they crumbled at the touch.

I observed that some of Sequoyah's alphabet resembled the English and I figured out that he had used it as a basis for his own invented syllabary. Thinking I might be able to teach myself to read and write in the solitude of my Mountaintop cabin by industrious, mechanical imitation, I began to copy word by word Parson Brownlow's *Whigs* and passages of his famous book. Sometimes I wished I could have broken out of that grinding concentration into a rush of Cherokee print. Here is a sample.

$$D \, \mathcal{S} \, \mathcal{Z} \mathcal{S} \; \sigma \, \sigma \, \psi \, W L \; \mathcal{S} \, \theta \, \Gamma \, \mathcal{A} \; Z \, L \, \hbar \; \mathcal{U} G \, \Gamma$$
$$\Theta \, \mathcal{G} \, \mathcal{S} \; \mathcal{G} \, \hbar \, \theta \, J \, \mathcal{A} \, \mathcal{D} \, \mathcal{A} \; 4 \, M \; \mathcal{D} \, \mathcal{A} \; V \, \mathcal{S} \; D \, \mathcal{G} \, \mathcal{D}$$
$$\dagger \, \mathcal{Y} \theta \theta \; \sigma^{\!\!\!+} \, \mathcal{L} \, \theta \theta \, \Gamma^{\!\!\!-} \; \dot{R} \, V \, L \; \sigma \, \mathcal{D} \, \mathcal{D}^{\!\!\!-} \, \sigma \! + \; J \, \mathcal{S} \; \mathcal{G} \, W \, \hbar$$

All my experiences had been solely of the senses. When I learned to read and write, The Word became everything. As it must have for Sequoyah, and in different ways for Parson Brownlow. Some words I relished the look and sound of, breaking them into syllables. Words such as bom-bas-tic! cons-pir-acy! in-car-cer-ra-ted! musk-et-ball! in-cen-di-ary! vex-a-tion! combus-ti-ble! es-pouse! tem-pus fu-git! ex-cor-i-ate! ex-ci-ted me. As I began to know how to read aloud, I shouted the words I liked, down off the top of the Mountain.

I tried in very agony to read the Parson's *Whigs*, by fire-light as my Greatgrandfather had, but silently, though sometimes, as if I were gorged to spilling over, bursting into a roar, to bring Greatgrandfather back, and some of the *Whigs* fell apart in my hands.

As I struggled to learn to read and write, the smell of skins drying was in the room with me. I forgot the one-legged Yankee at Vicksburg and the old-young Rebel Sharpshooter in Pulaski.

That spring and summer, I sold enough skins so that I didn't have to finagle people into letting me draw their pictures. But I had done it so much before that people had seen my work on walls in houses in and around Elizabethton, so this fellow came up to me at the market house, and I was drawing him and attracting a crowd, when another man stepped up and looked over my shoulder.

"You draw well," he said, and I knew by his tone he was a minister. "Where did you study?"

Well, the answer to that question led over hill and dale to the fact that— and I admitted it—I could neither read or write very well, having no formal education at all. When I told him who my father was, he said, "Well, that satisfies me. Come to see me at Carter's Depot this evening and we'll talk about making you over into a gentleman and a scholar."

When I looked over my shoulder, he had turned his back to walk on, and the man I was drawing had to tell me the gentleman's name, Reverend William Blount Carter. I did not know then that he had been the Architect of the plan to burn the bridges on the Grand Trunk Line through the Great Valley of Tennessee, the plan that led me to go off to join the army in '61. Later, I learned that no one else knew either.

When I went to see him as a beginning student, I was almost as nervous as when I went off to the War.

"I knew your Greatgrandfather, your grandfather, and your father," he told me, having set me down in his library. "As a tribute to them, I want to help one of their surviving kin. Can you come down off Holston often enough this summer to learn to read and write proficiently? I am speaking of hard work of a kind different from what you are obviously used to."

I said I *could* do it, I *wanted* to do it, and *would* do it. I craved to read my Greatgrandfather's books and Brownlow's *Whigs* without agony.

By September, I could read aloud from *Pilgrim's Progress* to Reverend Carter's satisfaction and my own.

WHEN AT THE FIRST I TOOK MY PEN IN HAND
THUS FOR TO WRITE, I DID NOT UNDERSTAND
THAT I AT ALL SHOULD MAKE A LITTLE BOOK

In such a mode; nay, I had undertook
To make another; which, when almost done,
Before I was aware, I this begun.

John Bunyan! bless him.

~ I read like a house afire, till my head was full of books. I sat in that cabin on the Mountaintop and started thinking and couldn't stop. I went through Brownlow's *Whigs* and *Parson Brownlow's Book* like greased lightning. After I read Brownlow's narrative I was able to remember my own actions in the War more clearly.

Parson Brownlow's voice was the one I had grown up listening to. I tracked down his six other books, which were long debates on religion, slavery, and politics, including his autobiography, that he wrote when he was only twenty-eight.

Even when I read aloud, it was not my own voice, nor Brownlow's— which I actually heard once only—but my Greatgrandfather's voice, turning Brownlow's editorials into orations, spiked with Highland sayings, anecdotes, and tall tales.

Reading Doctor Ramsey's *Annals of Tennessee,* always silently, I heard the voice of Grandfather History, not Doctor Ramsey's voice, but my Greatgrandfather's meditative inner voice, that I had heard only in my imagination, of course, as I looked at him, sitting pensive before the same "place of fire" where he roared Brownlow's pulp and print into combustible spirals of rhetoric and slam-bang invective.

Books, yes, I have read, for the facts mostly, but I have listened now to many voices in the past thirty years, and my own, and they overmaster books.

Reading Parson Brownlow's diatribes I was struck by the idea that if I were to write my own autobiography at the same age Parson Brownlow did, twenty-eight, I could get all the facts of my life on a solitary piece of foolscap and call it *I Forget.* But one day, I decided that if I told even that much to my editor friend, I might start to remember more.

"Who is this man who offers this book to the world?" Parson Brownlow had asked, rhetorically. I put that question directly to myself, reluctant to submit the results to the world.

And so in the fall of 1876, I at twenty-eight began to join that vast legion of war memorialists. After I had told my story to my editor friend and re-read it as he had written it down for me, I re-wrote the first few pages in Cherokee, then translated them into English, and after that wrote in basic English, words so alive they seemed to bark back at me. As a word *described,* it excited me more than *what* I described. Sometimes I looked up the original Latin of a word, like feeling the warmth of the original pulse of a burning coal, and I would use the Latin. I restored the English for "My Story" and put in other things. Even as I employed my elementary ability to write, I heard voices always, never felt I was writing for cold type. Then I imagined listeners, readers, and silenced myself and swore my editor friend to secrecy.

Reverend Carter's Vision of the Burning of the Bridges

HAVING TOLD "MY STORY" IN 1876 AND REWRITTEN IT, I WAS MADE restless by a sense of so much missing. Daily hunting and trapping somehow made me more sharply aware of the vacant places in my story.

Although he knew nothing of my story and certainly had no inkling of my service in the Rebel army, Reverend Carter must have felt that something was missing in my life, and, I sensed, in his own, because when we met in the courthouse square one day, he asked me to come by and see him that very evening, as if, having at last made up his mind about something, he felt a certain urgency.

"I hold an orange in my hand, tilted, and a conception of it in my head."

I sat beside his desk.

"The orange becomes a globe, and the globe becomes an orange. What began as an actual orange in my left hand and a conception in my brain—separate phenomena—become, through a willed act of imagination, a single phenomenon.

"I *will* the spike of South Africa, dipping into my palm where the South Pole rests snug. I look down on the North American hemisphere as it curves westward. The North Pole is the navel. Distinguishing the Appalachian Mountains from the rest of the skin is difficult. But I *know* they are there. Without pivoting my hand on my wrist, I know the Pacific Ocean, China, India, Russia, Persia, Africa, the Atlantic Ocean, Europe are there. Maps my eyes have scanned, etched into memory, caress, like the lifelines of my palm, the orange's skin."

The peelings lay at his elbow. The scent of the skin made me aware of my nostrils. The tip of my tongue vibrated.

"As school children memorize 'Horatio at the Bridge,' *I* memorize, by virtue of sufficiently repeated contact, maps. I can call maps to mind, even their colors, but what comes when I deliberately try to *see* are not printed names, rather actual rivers and creeks and mountains and railroads and towns, simultaneously. Towns we have never seen, that we visit in dreams, are composites of towns we *have* seen. Awake, I *will* what dreams involuntarily deliver, and see landscapes and towns I have never actually visited."

Keeping half, he handed me half of the orange. We ate in silence. We spit seeds into our cupped hands.

"I will draw you a map of the Great Valley of East Tennessee."

I watched his steady hand draw a map of the Great Valley from upper Alabama to lower Virginia.

"Now, I must swear you to secrecy. Very few of our East Tennessee Unionists know what I am about to reveal to you. Even your own family did not know. Only their leader knew. But some of my nine raid leaders are turning against me. I have chosen you—to tell the truth some day, after I am gone, in every detail. I was the Architect of the Master Plan to Burn the Bridges. On *that* night, I looked at the map and saw nine distinct bridges burning."

Nine? The bridge my family burned was not the only one? I did not interrupt. He was telling me what he had called me there to hear.

"General McClellan saw with perfect railroad executive's vision.

"President Lincoln saw a snake that strangles, a crown of thorns, a laurel wreath.

"Parson Brownlow saw words at last become burning flesh.

"General Thomas saw what *ought* to be done.

"General Samuel Powhatan Carter, my brother, saw cavalry mobility, access to East Tennessee.

"General Sherman saw only the lack of rails for supply or retreat north."

"I, the first time I saw a map of the valley," I told Reverend Carter, "wondered where the mountains had gone."

"Hovering over my map, I hear the voices of:

"General Samuel Carter, thinking of me, 'My brother is in motion now, while I must squat here, and not budge until Sherman orders me.'

"General Thomas, 'I am ready. The president is ready. General McClellan is ready. Reverend Carter is ready. God is ready. Sherman wavers.'

"President Lincoln, 'We have betrayed them, sir. There are all kinds of treason. Sometimes the president is most liable.'

"Senator Andrew Johnson, 'They will be hunted, and caught, and hanged. And my wife and Reverend Carter's are captive in that place.'

"General Sherman, 'It will not do to advance far into Tennessee.'

"General McClellan, 'I did everything but beg Buell. By God, didn't I indeed beg that man?'

"President Lincoln, 'General Buell, have arms gone forward for East Tennessee?'

"General Buell, 'My judgment from the first has been decidedly against it.'

"General Sherman, 'Recollect that East Tennessee is my horror.'"

"Over the years," I said, trying to contribute to the invigorating line of thought Reverend Carter had laid down, "I have stumbled onto or sought out facts, rumors, testimonials, like artifacts scattered over a battlefield, concerning the burning of the bridges. It seemed as if that event had gotten lost among the multitude of historical writings."

"And so, one day," Reverend Carter went on, oblivious, "I gave in to a powerful urge to collect all the elements and shape them into a purely factual, historical account, with the intention of offering the article to *The Atlantic Monthly* or *The North American Review* or some other national publication. Allow me to read to you some of what I wrote.

"'I was the Architect of the Master Plan.

"'At midnight, on November 8, 1861, in Mr. Crow's house on Emory River, 2 or 3 miles from Kingston, my command post, about 25 miles from the railroad bridge over the Tennessee River at Loudon, the second most important on the line, almost exactly at midpoint, I imagined, for over the hundredth time, a Confederate train, loaded with troops, arms, salt, bacon, setting out from Stevenson, Alabama, to supply the Confederate Army (not yet commanded by General Lee), crossing nine bridges on the 270-mile Grand Trunk Line through the Great Valley of East Tennessee to Bristol, which straddles the Tennessee-Virginia line.

"'I envisioned a small band of Union Mountaineer raiders poised near the high, long railroad bridge over the Tennessee River at Bridgeport, Alabama, another near the two bridges over Chickamauga Creek east of Chattanooga, a third band close to the bridge over the Hiawassee River at Charleston, Tennessee, a fourth only twenty-five miles from my command post—the long bridge over the Tennessee at Loudon, a fifth band east of Knoxville near the long bridge over the Holston River at Strawberry Plains, a small band of raiders near the bridge over Lick Creek, west of Greeneville, a seventh between the bridge over the Watauga River at Carter's Depot and the bridge over the Holston River at Union just west of Bristol, ready to put the torch to each wooden railroad bridge, each band attacking at exactly the same moment, while General George H. Thomas simultaneously was to invade the Confederacy through Cumberland Gap to seize the rail center at Knoxville, in the first railroad war in history.

"'Having conceived the plan and imagined the many possibilities in its execution, I, who, owing to an old lingering, debilitating ailment, had not assigned to myself one of the bridges, had an omniscient vision of the seven bands of East Tennessee Mountain Unionists simultaneously striking nine targets—victories and a possible defeat or two all along the 270-mile line—and felt their energies and various emotions of fear, ferocity, and elation concentrated in myself.

"'In my omniscience—natural to a Presbyterian minister—'"

Here he interrupted the reading with a laugh, but I was taking the word "omniscience" seriously.

"'I saw Old Fort Loudon, the first English Fort in the Southwest, erected in 1756, only 12 miles below the Loudon Bridge where the pioneer spirit sprang up out of the blood of soldiers and their families whom the Cherokees, their captors, massacred, saw Sycamore Shoals on the Watauga River where civilization west of the Appalachians began to develop—where the first permanent American settlement outside the original thirteen colonies was established, where the Watauga Association—the first majority-rule system of American democratic government—was instituted in 1772, where the largest private or corporate real estate transaction (over two million acres) in American history was made between prominent settlers and the Cherokee Indians, where John Sevier led the defense of white settlers against attacks by Old Abram of Chilhowee at Fort Watauga, where in 1780 the Overmountain men assembled to attack and defeat the British at King's Mountain, a decisive battle in the Revolutionary War in the South. The autumn-stripped sycamores outside reminded me of that old name for Elizabethton, Sycamore Shoals, county seat of Carter County, which my grandfather Landon Carter renamed after his wife, Elizabeth McLin.

"'I was full, at that midnight moment, of a sense of my own history. My greatgrandfather, John Carter, a Virginian, a Cavalier by descent, one of the first settlers of the Watauga region, president of the Council of Five which administered the Watauga Association, the first free representative government in the Mississippi Valley.'

"'The Carters married into another prominent family in the region, the Taylor clan, picking up the blood of Pocahontas that made the women renowned for their beauty and the men remarkable for their striking dark faces. The uncle who gave me my name was president of the Constitutional Convention of Tennessee in 1834 and was three times a member of Congress.'"

I reveled in exposure to the workings of Reverend Carter's history-imbued mind and sensibility.

"'My parents wanted me to serve in the Presbyterian ministry. I went from Presbyterian Washington College at Limestone (where many influential Tennesseans, including my older brother, Samuel Powhatan Carter, and my younger brother, James P. T. Carter, were educated) to Princeton seminary. As minister of a church at Rogersville, about fifty miles west of Elizabethton, between Clinch and Pine Mountains on the Holston River, I was known for the style of my sermons: terse, lucid, compact, forceful. My voice was soft, some said musical. I was tall, straight, slender, and moved gracefully. My neat, elegant dress, my dark, foreign look—'"

I was impatient to hear about the burning of the bridges, even though I wanted to know about his family and himself, the history that led up to the burning.

"'—delicate features, bright eyes, peculiar smile caused men to gaze at me, according to Judge Temple's own words in a book on which he has been working, *Notable Men of East Tennessee*. Ill health forced me to retire from the ministry and manage my family's extensive farms. When our father, Alfred, died, James managed the iron foundry, and Samuel made a career in the Navy.'"

I wished I could give such an account of my own family and myself— if only, for a start, *to* myself.

"'I kept up the Whig tradition of all the Carters and Taylors when I spoke against the evils of secession, 'with the intensity,' Judge Temple writes, 'of an ancient oracle or a Hebrew prophet.' I supported the most extreme measures of the Greeneville convention on June 1. On July 1, 1861, just before the election to go with or against the Union, I went into Kentucky as a refugee, probably the second person to flee Carter County, my intention being to persuade Federal authorities to rescue Loyal East Tennesseans. I convinced General Thomas, who convinced General Sherman, saying 'The destruction of the Grand Trunk Railroad through Tennessee would be the most important service that could be done for the country.' General Thomas sent me up to Washington, where General McClellan, Secretary of State Seward, and President Lincoln approved my plan to burn the bridges.'"

Eager to hear his natural voice again, I asked Reverend Carter, "What were your thoughts on the night of the raids?"

"Keep Carter County as much like frontier, and wilderness, as we can, for as long as we can. The railroad takes us east, if and when we want to go. But wasn't wilderness what we came for? The railroad is there and it is good for Carter County. But right now, it must burn, like a string. I strike here, far from home, but in striking here, I, through others, my agents, strike there—Lucifer to the Secessionists, Archangel Michael to the Unionists. To protect my 'holy ground,' where my ancestors created a nation. The Switzerland of America, Parson Brownlow called it. Gateway to the Smokies. From preacher to saboteur, and only forty-one. At Greeneville Convention that summer, Representative Nelson called me a fire-eater. Nelson was arrested before he could reach Washington to serve the loyal people who voted his victory in July.

"I am far from Carter County now, I thought. First Cincinnati. Johnson and Maynard constantly appealing to the president for help. Then I had to go myself. Washington in September, like being inside a boil, if a boil could raise not only heat, but dust, too. The capitol dome unfinished, the nation dismantled. Lincoln compassionately predisposed to invade, but hard work trying to persuade the others, each possessed by his own scheme. Lincoln called my own 'A Grand Scheme,' to destroy what General Mc-Clellan, that excellent railroad man turned Napoleon, calls 'The Grand Trunk Line.'"

Listening to Reverend Carter's voice, I saw trains stalled on bridges, steam drifting across broken track, fog below on the river.

"General Thomas was poised now to invade. And with him, my brothers Samuel and James, all those who fled to Kentucky ready now to return with fire, all waiting near Camp Dick Robinson for orders from Thomas to move into Carter County, all killing their way home to stop other killing. Much, very much depends upon this raid. The plans concealed under my wife's dress as she passed over five of the bridges on the East Tennessee and Virginia Railroad to reach Captain David Fry, in charge of operations above Knoxville. 'I must go up into Virginia, General,' she would say, 'to visit my wounded son.' So we can wound or kill tonight some other mother's sons. Merciless patterns.

"I looked into the palm of my left hand, seeing 270 miles of track from Bridgeport up to the bridge over the Holston at Union, all the streams and bridges, the guards, and the motive power of the lines, the rolling stock, the fire-headed locomotives, and six bands of men, each led by my carefully picked agents, each man's belly and brain alive with fire. The hoarse whispering of men who started out with colds and men getting or in danger of getting colds. Cold heads and hands and feet, but in their hearts, bellies, and brains—fire! As I imagined fire catch at the long Bridgeport Bridge, I felt as if I were firing all nine at once, creating a lake that burned with fire and brimstone, and 'the wailings of the damned ghosts' of Davis and his crew 'will rise,' as Parson Brownlow wrote, 'upon the flames.'

"But as I imagined the first and most important victory at Bridgeport, Alabama, two raiders found a heavy guard there, at the longest and most powerfully built of the nine bridges, and watched a supply train from the cotton states on the Memphis and Charleston railroad cross the Tennessee River and enter lower East Tennessee. They rode back to their home, 80 miles north, to keep a secret that in their case was an empty gesture."

As he set his manuscript aside, I was thrilled to realize that my eager listening had quickened the tongue of the teller.

"About 50 miles north of the burning bridge at Calhoun, I handed the map to Captain William Cross of Scott County, one of the two Federal army officers detailed to assist me.

"'Everybody got a map like this?'

"'Captain Cross, no one needs a map. The lines on their palms ain't no less familiar. This is just to hold, in satisfaction. One glance, one stroke, one swift ride, nine bridges. Fire on a line 270 miles from Bridgeport, Alabama, to Bristol, Virginia. Satisfaction. Look. Don't you feel it?'

"'I do, Reverend, I do.'

"'But *they* don't need none. Each man's torch—I hope each man bears a torch—lights his own fuse. Fire smoldering *in* each of them, and the fire in each burns for others, too, who can't ride with them, as I cannot. Imagine.'

"'Oh, trust me to imagine, Reverend.'

"'Maybe I will, and maybe I won't. But I do trust you to do your job well. We are the fire that goes before the army of deliverance.'

"'How many trains, Reverend, on this line right now between Bridgeport and Bristol, do you reckon?'

"'As many as you like to imagine.'

"As the captain left Mr. Crow's house to meet ten men along the way to the bridge, dogs barking at Captain Cross excited my blood.

"'Burning those bridges only two days after they elected their renegade president,' said Mr. Crow, 'will have a demoralizing effect on them and inspire our own people.' Sensing my need to be alone, Mr. Crow left my room.

"As A. M. Cate and his brothers and their friends attacked the four bridges to the south, Captain Cross found that long bridge, second most important of the nine targeted, over the Tennessee River at Loudon, forbiddingly well-guarded. Retreating, he must have known with regret that I was imagining the most crucial victory of all there."

The Architect of the Grand Plan, I thought, probably imagined then, as I do now, the supply train passing over the lower bridges. And nobody aboard has any sense of having eluded catastrophe behind, nor of approaching possible catastrophe ahead.

"Thirty-five miles northeast of the Loudon Bridge, the train approaches Knoxville, the major city on the line, enters the station General Thomas's federal troops were to have already seized, and then I had an odd vision:

directly on the opposite side of the globe from Knoxville and the Valley of East Tennessee, a windstorm, I imagined, was rising up out of the uninhabited wasteland, surrounded by mountains, of the Makan Desert in Western China."

With him, I was in awe of the way the human imagination leaps about on its own.

"Fire in its head, as if the fire in the furnace had a will of its own, the locomotive moves along its trajectory toward the long bridge over the Holston River at Strawberry Plains in Jefferson County, fifteen miles east of Knoxville, the railroad's name having changed now to the East Tennessee and Virginia.

"What I and the men in my seven raiding parties did not know, had not even imagined, was that General Thomas had not advanced beyond Crab Orchard, Kentucky. I did not know that my brother, Lieutenant Samuel Carter and the legion of East Tennesseans who had made the hazardous trek over the mountains into Eastern Kentucky to participate in Lincoln's promised invasion were ordered to stop. Infuriated, disillusioned, they had been forced to abandon their own people to their vindictive Confederate neighbors and to marauders in the Rebel army.

"Ignorant of the change of plan ordered by Sherman, the bands of bridge burners had struck. Now they were forced to hide or to escape into Kentucky as best they could. An episode, not as famous but strategically just as ineffective as the Great Locomotive Chase below Chattanooga, in the first railroad war in history passed into relative obscurity."

Talk, Reverend Carter, I suppressed a compulsion to plead, about the burning of the Lick Creek Bridge where they hanged my brother, Tim. I was afraid he would draw me out about my own role there and my Rebel service later in the War.

"Even as I was writing this article about the bridge burning, I suspected I was failing, and after I had reread it, I was certain I had failed, to shut out whatever was not pure fact. I knew that editors would instruct me to expunge all fanciful elements. I set it aside, but could never, somehow, work up enough interest to reduce what I had written to the status of an unimpeachable historical account."

"Here's a fact you could have recorded," I said, hopeful he would revise to make the article publishable so I could read it and meditate on it.

"When the *Sultana* exploded, several bridge burners were among the drowned and the survivors."

It hurt me that Reverend Carter only smiled and nodded, then told me about the scene in *Harper's Weekly* where we see Colonel David Fry swear the bridge burners to secrecy. Then he showed the newspaper to me.

Turn to page 325 of your copy of *Harper's Pictorial History of the Civil War* and you will see for yourself a large engraving of that scene, "Unionists of East Tennessee Swearing by the Flag," reprinted from the March 1892 edition. Not *my* sketch. I am not good enough to sell to magazines, even if I knew how to go about it. The interior looks like my own cabin here on Holston (in fact, I used it for my own drawing), longjohns on the line high up under the slanting roof, among the smoke fumes from the fireplaces like the one Greatgrandfather sat by to read Parson Brownlow, a-shouting. The flag draped over the table, everybody's hands on it, a candle in a bottle illuminating the faces crowded around, right arms uplifted. I look into this sketch, trimmed over the top like an arch or a dome, feeling as if I am inside Mathew Brady's "What's-it" wagon, looking out through the mask-like eyelets at the candlelit, shadowed scene no photography by Brady could have caught in that dim light, even though it looks alive, like a photograph.

Am *I* the Man Who Shot General Sanders?

ONE SLEETY MARCH DAY ON SOUTH HOLSTON, I WAS HUNTING, THAT DAY not for skins but for food. I was feeling faint from hunger and chill, when I saw my supper walking toward me like he was looking at *his* supper. When the bear saw me, it recognized me for a human and turned and dropped to all fours to get away from me, and I propped my rifle on a branch and got it in my sights just as it got too far for good aim and wished I had my Sharps rifle with the telescopic lens, and that's when I got a general in my cross-hairs, riding a white horse up the pike toward the house where I stood at one of the tower windows aiming down at him.

Something, the light, the way the bear had ambled toward me, the way I felt, a little feverish from exposure to rain and sleet, and fatigued from rambling up and down the Mountainside, hungry, had brought it back. I was in a tower and two men were shot and one was dead and seven others had run out, but none of them was that old-looking man who had held still for me to draw his face in Pulaski as he told me about shooting General Sanders. He had proved out to be one of that tribe of liars the war had spewed up.

I had shot a General. But was it a *fact* that I had shot General *Sanders*, the man they named the fort after, the fort we attacked in Knoxville?

After I talked to a few people down in Elizabethton, I was pretty sure it was Sanders because only one general was killed in that battle.

The voices, and daily walking, tracking game on the Mountain, threw up repeatedly the question, Why, if I am the Sharpshooter who shot General William Price Sanders (and I am now almost certain that I am), did I feel then, as I do still, that I missed the War?

Out hunting, after that day, I found only General Sanders in my sights and I broke out in a feverish sweat every time. The sense of having missed everything else kept me in night sweats.

So I fled the Mountain to find the war again.

The War on Target

Retracing My Steps

During the year 1876–77, I retraced my steps, moving toward whatever I might discover, trying to get the War, as I experienced it, on target. I needed to work my way to the Bleak House tower in Knoxville, but I did not start with Lick Creek Bridge and "Castle Fox" Prison. Instead, I moved up the Valley of Virginia.

Bearded men, like the Ancient Mariner, who were often only in their late twenties, accosted me. That happenstance of the one-legged Yankee asking me to sketch him into my drawing of the crater at Vicksburg earned me enough money to keep me on the move, because it encouraged me to sketch veterans at the scenes of battle, for many lived nearby the places where they fought, especially in the Shenandoah Valley, where their memories were of serving in Stonewall Jackson's foot cavalry. I sketched them from their photographs, too, for themselves or for their widows, or for sons and daughters, bereft. I listened to storytellers.

I sketched the bridge at Union that my neighbors helped burn in '61, with John Taylor, who claims he helped burn it, standing on it.

And I crossed over into Bristol, Virginia, still not much more than a busy railroad center, where I had camped with General Longstreet.

And I wandered up the Valley of Virginia. Abingdon. Marion. Wytheville. Newbern. Christiansburg. Salem.

Last night as I rode into Lexington, my own shadow, frozen on the wall of a church, scared the wits out of me. It was gigantic, and when it did not move as I moved, my scalp burned. I rode away from it at a panic gallop and spent the night in the burned ruins of the Virginia Military Institute.

A man explained the mystery of the shadow of rider-and-horse on the church wall. In the shop window of a photographer hangs a glass plate of his famous photograph of General Lee mounted on Traveler. One night each month, the moon falls through a skylight and strikes the glass plate and projects onto the wall of the church across the street that fantastic shadow of Lee and Traveler.

The college building sits magnificently on a hill, with a wide row of enormous white columns. President Lee, they tell me, would come downstairs from his office in the central building and walk between the columns down a neat brick path to the church he ordered built.

Lee is buried in the basement of Lee Episcopal Chapel on the campus of Washington and Lee University. Traveler is buried on the east side, facing north. Go see.

A student I met had by heart what General Lee told the students when he became the college's president. "I have led the young men of the South to battle. I have seen many of them die on the field. I shall devote my remaining energy to training young men to do their duty in life."

For that speech I swapped him what Reverend Carter told me—Sherman's farewell to his students in Alexandria at the Louisiana Military Seminary, where he was its first superintendent. The students who had gathered to bid him farewell were weeping and Sherman was weeping, but he managed to say, "I cannot deliver the speech I had intended. The thought that I may be forced to kill some of you horrifies me." Putting his hand on his heart, he said, "You are all here," turned on his heel and left the room.

As I left Lexington, I visited General Jackson's grave in the Presbyterian cemetery.

At Sharpsburg a man offers me a room in which to pass the night. The next morning, he shows me Alexander Gardner's portfolio of photographs.

A Photographic Sketchbook of The Civil War it's called, actual positive prints—each pasted in place. A very expensive book published in Washington in 1866 by the photographer himself. Strange that he entitles it a "sketchbook."

Several of the photographs were missing, including HOME OF A REBEL SHARPSHOOTER, GETTYSBURG, July 1863, but I read Gardner's commentary, printed on the page opposite, and saw the missing photo clearly. I copied the passage in my sketchbook.

"On the Fourth of July, 1863, Lee's shattered army withdrew from Gettysburg, and started on its retreat from Pennsylvania to the Potomac. From Culp's Hill, on our right, to the forests that stretched away from Round Top, on the left, the fields were thickly strewn with Confederate dead and wounded, dismounted guns, wrecked caissons, and the debris of a broken army.

"The artist, in passing over the scene of the previous days' engagements, found in a lonely place the covert of a Rebel sharpshooter, and photographed the scene presented here. The Confederate soldier had built up between two rocks, a stone wall, from the crevices of which he had directed his shots, and, in comparative security, picked off our officers.

"The side of the rock on the left shows, by the little white spots, how our Sharpshooters and infantry had endeavored to dislodge him. The trees in the vicinity were splintered, and their branches cut off, while the front of the wall looked as if just recovering from an attack of geological small-pox.

"The sharpshooter had evidently been wounded in the head by a fragment of shell which had exploded over him, and had laid down on his blanket to await death. There was no means of judging how long he had lived after receiving his wound, but the disordered clothing shows that his suffering must have been intense.

"Was he delirious with agony, or did death come slowly to his relief, while memories of home grew dearer as the field of carnage faded before him? What visions, of loved ones far away, may have hovered above his stony pillow! What familiar voices may he not have heard, like whispers beneath the roar of battle, as his eyes grew heavy in their long, last sleep!

"On the nineteenth of November, the artist attended the consecration of the Gettysburg Cemetery, and again visited the 'Sharpshooter's Home.' The musket, rusted by many storms, still leaned against the rock, and the skeleton of the soldier lay undisturbed within the moldering uniform, as did the cold form of the dead, four months before. None of those who went up and down the fields to bury the fallen had found him.

"'Missing,' was all that could have been known of him at home, and some mother may yet be patiently watching for the return of her boy, whose bones lie bleaching unrecognized and alone, between the rocks at Gettysburg."

I expected that I would sooner or later run across that photograph. In the meantime, something about Gardner's description struck a false note. Union soldiers would have taken that rifle; had they failed to see it, relic hunters would have found it, and then burial details would have disposed of the body. That and more made me feel queasy.

Freezing at Burnside's Bridge on Sharpsburg battlefield, I sketch it. Named after Burnside because he insisted through storms of blood on holding it, only to learn later that there was a shallow crossing close by, just as General Longstreet later misjudged the depth of the ditch in front of Fort Sanders, commanded by Burnside.

On my way north to Gettysburg, I came across a newspaper sketch made from Gardner's photograph. I copied the sketch into my sketchbook.

In Gettysburg, a man who caught a glimpse of my sketch of the Sharpshooter tells me he has seen the actual photograph in Alexander Gardner's *A Photographic Sketchbook of the Civil War*. He described its mood so sharply, I saw it myself and carried it around in my head as I wandered the field.

I stood facing the very place in Devil's Den where the man says Gardner shot the photograph, calling it "Home of a Rebel Sharpshooter," on July 6, 1863. Massive boulders on each side of him, the young Rebel soldier built a stone wall between.

Having sketched the actual site of the dead Sharpshooter's nest (or photographed it, to reverse Gardner's figure of speech when he called his photograph a "sketch"), I looked again closely at my own sketch of the sketch that was made from the photograph for the newspaper. I now know what is wrong with it. That rifle is not a Sharpshooter's rifle.

As I walked north along Seminary Ridge, it occurred to me that I had not sketched the Peach Orchard, the Wheatfield, the Valley of Death, the Slaughter Pen and its "Harvest of Death," the Little Round Top or Big Round Top, or even the house where John Burns, "the Old Patriot" who jumped into the battle, lived, because I was distracted by a tendency of my eyes to stare like a camera lens at scenes, and walk away with the photograph developing slowly in my brainpan.

Talking with people, I tried to lead up to the photograph. A man who fell in walking with me on Seminary Ridge told me it was Timothy O'Sullivan who took the Sharpshooter photograph that Gardner took credit for and that the public often attributed to Mathew Brady.

Coming back south, along Cemetery Ridge, another man told me he watched photographers on July 6 and 7 drag bodies from a field, where they had been laid out in rows for burial, to a giant, rugged rock where they made them to look as if the those dead had fallen in battle.

Out of nowhere, a memory came over me. I am walking a battlefield. Miraculously, among the corpses left three days unburied in the sun, a man's chest heaves, inhaling, exhaling. As I stepped over the corpse nearest him to offer words of encouragement, I saw that it was only maggots, foaming at his lips, and stumbled backward over the other corpse.

I stood where Pickett made the charge. I try to see it. The action freezes, like storm waves in a painting of the sea. Light, as in a painting, caught.

Men with stories watch me, prowl around me, and even before they can utter them, I hear their voices, telling it, Yankee voices—although many of *us* came down originally from Pennsylvania, as Boone did from the Brandywine River, to settle in the Valley of Virginia or the Great Valley of Tennessee.

The inevitable local "guide" tells me that the Wesley Culp boy, coming home with "Stonewall's Brigade" as a Rebel invader, was killed on Culp Hill at Gettysburg (after a secret visit to his sisters, and having promised to return). That could have happened to *me*.

And another man told me the sad story of twenty-year-old Jennie Wade. She was staying with her sister Mrs. McClellan who had just had a baby three days earlier. As Jennie was baking bread, probably thinking of her fiancé, Corporal Skelly, who might also be engaged at that moment in a battle elsewhere, but who was in fact, unknown to her, dying of wounds received in a battle at Winchester, Virginia, she was shot in the back and died instantly of a stray Confederate sniper's bullet that had penetrated two doors. She was the only civilian killed in the battle. About a week later, her fiancé, who never heard of her death, died of his wounds.

I hang on every word of such stories, hoping one of them, or all of them

together, will, one of these days, fix me in my own place in the war. But I
feel, in the moment of the telling, too sharply the fate of the victims of
irony to fit myself into the picture.

Dodging a fusillade of words and images, I got on the road to South
Mountain, Maryland.

From Manassas to Knoxville

I GO ON DOWN INTO VIRGINIA TO MANASSAS. THAT'S WHERE WILMER McLean's house, "Yorkshire," once stood, at McLean's Ford, that he had bought, seeking rural tranquillity, and that was shattered in the first Bull Run battle, for it became General Beauregard's headquarters, and a shell fell down the chimney and exploded in the stew. So Mr. McLean moved as far as he could get from this war, isolating himself and his family at Appomattox Courthouse, giving him cause later to say, "The War began in my front yard and ended in my parlor," where General Lee surrendered to Grant.

I sit my horse at the crossroads of the turnpike and Mountain Road and go over again in my own imagination what I've been told over and over and remember hearing about even when I was here with General Longstreet. General Jackson sits on his horse alone. A. P. Hill, with a group of staff officers, rides up to him.

"Press them, cut them off from United States Ford, Hill. Press them!" General Jackson orders Captain Boswell to show General Hill the way.

A courier brought him a report from General Stuart. Then he followed General Hill at a little distance up Mountain Road. General Jackson and his staff got between the battleline of Lane's brigade and his skirmishers. He seemed to be trying to figure out possible actions to take.

He rode back toward the turnpike in advance of his men. General Hill rejoined him.

Major Barry mistook General Jackson and his staff and escort for Yankee cavalry and fired on them. All the men and horses with him fell to the ground, killed or wounded, except Stonewall Jackson, shot in wrist and arm, who stayed mounted on Little Sorrell, who, terrified, rushed in panic away from what he took to be the position of the enemy, but toward the actual enemy. A limb hit Jackson in the face, knocked off his cap (which mapmaker Hotchkiss retrieved, refused to return to Mrs. Jackson). Jackson used his wounded arm to pull the reins, to direct Little Sorrel back toward the road. One of his fallen staff rose, grabbed the reins, and General Jackson fell into his arms. They eased him down upon the ground.

A fellow told me that at an asylum in Baltimore someone told a lunatic walking behind the fence of Jackson's death. He staggered, dazed, weak with sadness, in circles, then stopped, a light coming over his face. "Oh, what a battle must have been raging in Heaven, when the archangel of the Lord needed the services of Stonewall Jackson!" But what most people have come to know is not that man but the many poems and eulogies.

At Guiney Station, standing in the small house where General Jackson died, I imagined his dying words, "Let us cross over the river and rest in the shade of the trees."

I returned to the Wilderness, where, almost exactly a year to the day after and only four miles away from the same spot where Stonewall Jackson was shot, General Longstreet, while I was up that burning tree sharpshooting, was shot in the throat. Moments before they were shot by their own men, both Jackson and General Longstreet were exhilarated with victory.

When he marched on Knoxville, General Longstreet was already wounded in spirit by Bragg's disrespect and by self-inflicted blows and he received and inflicted upon himself more such wounds throughout the War and after, but not until May 4, 1864, in the Wilderness campaign was he wounded physically. Not a scratch at Knoxville, amid one of the most ignominious defeats of the War, not even as he reconnoitered in plain view of enemy Sharpshooters with Generals Leadbetter, Alexander Porter, and Micah Jenkins at Mabry's Hill. Not until he had once again proven to Hancock at the Wilderness what he had been famous for. Then, he exposed himself needlessly, aggressively, recklessly, like Zollicoffer, Jackson, A. P. Hill, Nelson, and Winthrop (his dash on a white horse was a reckless exaggeration of them all) in front of Bleak House, and General Sanders, and even like General Lee, who in the heat of battle started to lead a charge, until his own infantry's shouts of "General Lee to the rear!" restored his usual cool-headedness.

On the second day of the battle, I see the Wilderness woods on fire, and in them the wounded roasted, screaming, muted to General Longstreet, who was already slightly deaf. Old Pete had just conferred with Generals Micah Jenkins and Kershaw (who had been with him downstairs at Bleak House), and those who fell back, talking of victory, especially Jenkins, who had despaired for the Confederacy until General Longstreet's brilliant move that day in sending four brigades in a flank attack from behind an unfinished railroad embankment. General Longstreet rode ahead on Plank Road toward Brock Road.

Wofford's and "Tige" Anderson's men (Wofford and Anderson had walked downstairs at Bleak House, too) had just entrenched on the left side of the road, unknown to Mahone's men, who turned to take position on the right side and mistook those on the left for Federals and fired on them.

General Longstreet, hearing firing from our positions, suggesting a mistake of some kind, breaking the rules for safety, rode ahead to stop the firing, got caught in crossfire, and a Minié ball went through his neck and crashed into his right shoulder, lifting him, I heard men say, out of his saddle, "like he was leaping up to look over a fence," and he fell back into the saddle, as Jenkin's brain caught a bullet (and tolerated it for an hour), and two "other" men (what *is* an "other" man?) fell dead. Shot in the crossfire by his own men.

It was Kershaw who yelled, "They are friends!" loud enough to stop the firing. Mahone's men, who poured into the road, were very sorry.

They set Old Pete against a tree. In the ambulance, Lee's Old Warhorse spit the blood out of his mouth so he could give an order. As he was being carried to the rear, he heard a soldier say, "He's dead, and they're telling that he's only wounded"—and Old Pete lifted his hat from off his pale face with his good hand—a greeting that a veteran might look forward to from Old Man Death himself, if he survived the Wilderness, if he succumbed of early wounds and old age, as General Longstreet himself did.

A man muttered at the scene, "He's master of the situation."

Although I did not see him downstairs at Bleak House, but heard his voice, I think now that I did *see* this shooting, without knowing who was getting shot.

General Lee's warhorse recovered, returned to duty six months later. To this day, he has never been able to speak above a whisper.

I talk to men everywhere I am. "Did you see *me* there?" I finally asked a one-armed man.

Many others talk of other battles at other places, for they, too, missed the battles in this neighborhood, as I did, even though I was actually here, somewhere. I am the mysterious figure in the background where men are gathered, who haunts the reunions, the consecrations, the conclaves of storytellers, I am "that feller over there" who has no story to tell, only the ones others have told me, I have only a hatfull of fragments to sort out. I am the very impulse without the tale.

I do not remember whether it ever occurred to me then that this War became important. It was just War.

I went on to Fredericksburg, and I am again at Mayre's House, which gives a panoramic view of the battlefield. "Over yonder," an idler points east, "is what we call Lee's Hill, where General Lee sat his horse with General Longstreet watching us mow down the great blue wave charging from the river through the burning town up toward the stone wall at the sunken road, and said, 'It is well that war is so terrible—we would grow too fond of it.'"

I can hear *him* say it.

Passing through Richmond with General Longstreet, I suppose I saw little of this city. I look very closely now at everything and recognize nothing. I walk among the ruins of the iron and munitions factories, the mills along the James River, factories that I never noticed, if I actually saw them, when we marched through here. Through blackened windows and holes, I catch glimpses of the Virginia State capitol building designed by Thomas Jefferson. I cross Kanawa Canal so I can look back at the city, see the capitol, splendid on the hill.

I am inside the capitol now, standing where, they tell me, Lee stood when he accepted command. An intuition of Lee's moment here swept over me just now, forcing stinging tears, and I shock myself. I sketched Lee saying, "Profoundly impressed with the solemnity of the occasion for which I must say I was not prepared, I accept the position assigned to me by your impartiality. I would have much preferred had your choice fallen on an abler man. Trusting in Almighty God, an approving conscience, and the aid of my fellow-citizens, I devote myself to the service of my native State, in whose behalf alone will I ever again draw my sword." My reverence for this man, called by one lady in this city "cold, quiet, and grand," does not satisfy me as explanation enough for these tears.

I sketched St. Paul's Church, where President Davis was worshipping when word of Lee's surrender at Appomattox Courthouse reached him, and St. John's Church, where Patrick Henry, who, they tell me, kept his wife in a cellar, where she died, raving, said, "Give Me Liberty or Give Me Death."

I sketched the prisons: Libby, Castle Thunder, and Belle Isle in the James River.

In a book store, I picked up *The Prison Life of Jefferson Davis*. The prison doctor wrote it. "Jefferson Davis was shackled" arrested my attention. Hanged, we all expected; imprisoned, we knew he was. The doctor reports that President Davis spoke of the comfort of a fire inside, cold wind and rain outside: "It had always appeared natural to him that savage nations, in the absence of revealed religion, should adopt fire as their god." What gave him the greatest discomfort in his cell was that hostile human eyes from three directions were continuously focussed upon him.

I sketched a great stone pyramid that the wives and mothers and sisters of the dead erected, each bringing a stone. The day is stunningly hot, but through the cracks between the stones issues an ice-house chill. They paid a sailor to place the last stone at the top. He fell to his death.

Here I sketched the Egyptian Building, the oldest medical building in the South, the only one still open during the War, the most perfect example of Egyptian architecture in the entire United States of America. The only one I have seen so far. Are there more on down the road? It is a shock to come upon it, unprepared. What they labelled "Authentic" hieroglyphics dominate the main lobby, remind me of Sequoyah's Cherokee syllabary.

Coming out, I noticed that the posts of the iron fence surrounding the building are shaped like mummy cases sticking out at the bottom to give the feet room.

I move on south to Petersburg, the town Grant besieged for ten months, filling the night sky with the most beautiful sight, one contraband Negro said, he had ever seen. The "dictator," an enormous Federal mortar bolted to a railroad flatcar, terrified the townspeople, as "Whistling Dick" had made nightmares of the lives of Union soldiers when Grant besieged Vicksburg.

I was somewhere else during that time, with General Longstreet. But many of the veterans I have met in and around Petersburg and as I wander the fields weren't here either; they talked of *other* battles, and only drawled the bare facts of this one, facts the citizens told them when they returned home.

I sketched the battlefield as it was then. And sure enough, one Rebel veteran wanted me to sketch him standing inside the Crater, even though he had not been there any more than *I* had. The explosion here was much greater than in the crater at Vicksburg. This time the Federals dug under Pegram's batteries, as the Rebels were digging a countermine. Burnside sent Hinks's Negro division in. Fifteen thousand troops, altogether, black and white. But the Rebels rallied and their batteries and mortars poured shells into the Crater, swarming with Yankees. That reminds me of the bloody ditch in front of Fort Sanders at Knoxville, where we were so severely exposed to enemy fire from the parapet above. Then General Mahone's cavalry charged the Yankees. Four thousand Yankees killed, wounded or captured, only 1,500 of ours. Long after the battle, 646 Union soldiers were dug up out of the Crater. Not one could be identified.

I wander Fort Hell and Fort Damnation and take a look at Meade's Station on Grant's military railroad where Lincoln met General Meade.

Like General Longstreet, Ambrose Powell Hill recklessly rode out in front of his own men. He was not shot by his own men, but he was rash and a little lost. Death by irony is a painful death, but it was, ironically, April 2, 1865, just after Grant's final assault at Petersburg, only days before General Lee's surrender at Appomattox that General Powell was shot by two Yankee stragglers who were as lost as he and his aide were.

General Lee wept. "He is at rest now, and we who are left are the ones to suffer." Then General Lee led the retreat across the Appomattox River.

The most fitting epitaph for Little Powell Hill would be what General Lee said on his own death bed five years later, "Tell Hill he *must* come up." But I take for my own General Lee's *last* words, "Strike the tent."

At the scene of other battles, even Petersburg, looking, sketching, listening, I often wonder, "Was *I* here? Sounds like what happened to me." But like me, most of the men never really knew what was happening around them, though nobody seems as misplaced in his mind and memory as *I* feel.

In Savannah, where Sherman ended his March to the Sea, and which he gave Lincoln as a Christmas present, I find a garden city, and a lack of sketch work. Sherman did not burn this city. It caught fire accidentally a few months after the surrender, and a hundred buildings perished.

Ahead of me lay Andersonville. To me during the War, a prison camp only, Andersonville to me and the world now. When I heard a few years ago that the prison's official name was Camp Sumter, I took the name to be a calculated derision of Fort Sumter, indirectly of Captain Anderson who surrendered that fort.

The anticipation of twilight at Andersonville filled me with such sadness I felt driven away from the very vicinity, north toward Atlanta.

Like Petersburg, and like Vicksburg and Knoxville, Atlanta had been besieged. The fire-king ruled on the day General Hood evacuated it. Atlanta was another major rail center, a manufacturing town that within twenty-five years has boomed into a metropolis, suffering and benefiting from war. I was never here with General Longstreet.

I wander the sprawling city, but it does not hold still, I can't see it as a city, nor feel that it is southern in any way. No river commerce. A city totally created around railroad depots. I do not like it.

I am taking the same route north toward Chattanooga that General Johnston took, retreating from Dalton slowly before Sherman's advance to Atlanta. In the summer of 1864, there were many separate battles within a few days around Kennesaw Mountain, but I see little evidence of battlements. Nature has reclaimed. And the railroad line is jittery with trains going to and from Atlanta. I pass through Altoona. I pass through Kingston.

I pass through Resaca. I have talked with men who fought here or elsewhere, all along the line. I sometimes try to tell it. But wherever I go, I cannot compete with all the voices.

"I think *this* happened, I'm not sure," I say. "Maybe that's just what somebody else told me about his own experiences," and their attention wanders.

In these places, along the bustling railroad, war and trains is *all* they have to talk about. The Great Locomotive Chase. Andrews, the spy, took over a Rebel train, The General, at Big Shanty and tried to steal it away to Chattanooga but was caught and hanged, with several others. It's a good story when you first hear it just above Atlanta, but as you get almost to Dalton you get almost hostile when the next one even looks like he wants to open his trap about the Great Chase. It's the perils of travel, I reckon.

The more I wandered—sketching and listening—the clearer the tower at Bleak House became, and the more clearly I remembered the places I have been to in my wandering, and the more clearly I saw the things I finally remember from the War while I was in those places.

In Stevenson, Alabama, I gaze upon the splendid bridge Reverend Carter's raiders failed to burn, the first on that 275-mile line.

I imagined all the bridges the raiders burned that night. I see only one Bridge, but it moves around ahead of me, and looks, is, different anywhere I cross it: the bridge that burned at Lick Creek, the bridge that didn't at Strawberry Plains that night, but that burned several times later on, the bridges at each point on the Grand Trunk Line. The Bridge goes up, is used, disappears, and reappears somewhere else.

Chattanooga is where we were dug in opposite Rosecrans when Bragg sent General Longstreet northeast to Knoxville. Here I did a sketch of two of the bridges, where they cross Chickamauga Creek as it loops, that Reverend Carter told me were burned as part of his Master Plan in 1861, the very hour when my folks were burning the bridge at Lick Creek. I didn't help burn that bridge, but I tried to remember—and did remember a great number—the many bridges I crossed, criss-crossing the regions of war, and the many officers crossing bridges who showed up in my telescopic sights.

I met one old fellow here, who reminds me he is only thirty-two, four years older than I am, but who walks like Greatgrandfather and who says, "I used to be so limber, I could bite off my own toe nail," walking with me over Chickamauga battlefield where he didn't fight himself, but where *we* arrived just in time to save our boys against Rosecrans.

"Let me tell you the story of a Sharpshooter at Petersburg, where *I* fought. We was all bored with the lack of action, so Bill jumped up and challenged any one of the Yankee Sharpshooters to a duel. 'I cannot be killed!' he yelled at them. I hear some Yankee painter made a picture of him standing there like that. Some Yankee lieutenant jumped up on their side and yelled back, 'I cannot be killed either!' They stood upon the works facing off at each other and fired, and our man dropped.

"The next morning, that same officer jumped up, like he had been waiting all night, a giant of a man, you could hardly miss hitting him, and yelled, 'I told you I could not be killed! Is there another man among you who wished to join his comrades in hell!'

"Sure. One of ours jumped up and the two of them took aim, and the Yankee giant lieutenant fell, and we all cheered.

"'Don't congratulate me,' said our Sharpshooter. 'I didn't fire a shot.'

"'No, *he* beat you to it!' said one man, pointing the finger at a feller grinning behind him.

"'Step out here!'

"Lieutenant Miller commanded ten of us to come to attention, and we shot the man, who was not a Sharpshooter, let me say, right there.

"'Send over the murderer of our lieutenant!' the Yankees were yelling; for they had figured out what happened, too.

"The Sharpshooter jumped up and called over to them, 'We just took care of the cowardly villain ourselves,' he yelled. 'Your lieutenant was a skillful and brave man!'

"That satisfied them, and us, too, but it soured us on Sharpshooter duels."

I did not tell him that I was a Sharpshooter here and on Lookout Mountain, because nothing here made me remember much more than what I have told in "My Story."

In Shiloh at Pittsburgh Landing where Buell's men came ashore and turned our victory into a retreat, I sketched Shiloh Church—there's always a church. My brother Jack and some of my neighbors must have seen it briefly in the surprise attack before they died.

As I stood in the Hornet's Nest on the Sunken Road, Burnside's Stone Bridge came to mind and I looked all over creation for it. Then it suddenly came over me that I had confused this Sunken Road with the Sunken Road at Antietam, combined with the woods on fire in the Wilderness. No one place will hold still to be only itself.

"Now here's Bloody Pond," said my guide, "where men came to drink and where we Sharpshooters ("we" the breed, not me personally, I was not in this battle) picked them off."

I tried to see blood, saw only clear water. It tastes sweet.

"Near the Peach Orchard, Bloody Pond, and the Hornet's Nest, General Albert Sidney Johnston impulsively yelled to his reluctant men at a decisive moment, 'I will lead you!'" said he of that brotherhood of informal battlefield guides. "A short while later, Governor Harris found him looking pale, reeling in his saddle under a white oak tree in a shallow ravine. Shot in the leg, an artery severed, his doctor having been earlier ordered, much against his will, to attend to wounded soldiers some distance away, General Johnston died within minutes.

"And here is where General Albert Sidney Johnston," said my guide, loving to ring off the full name again, "was shot. He was sitting on his horse, our 'fire-eater' Governor Isham Harris at his side."

The man asked me to sketch him sitting on the stump of the white oak tree that marks the spot. I begged off. I don't know why.

"We're in the Peach Orchard now," he said, and I was confused, for it was standing behind a peach tree that I had shot a mounted officer at Gettysburg, and for a moment I was in Gettysburg more keenly than I was in Shiloh.

"Right where we stand now," he said, "lie nine hundred soldiers in a trench grave."

My brother Jack among them?

We sat on one of the thirty Indian mounds in that area and shared what little I had to eat.

My guide kept unloading his store of anecdotes and curiosities. "I overheard a woman ask a veteran, 'What does it *mean* when they say a man was "missing?"'" and the vet replied, "'Missing' always means dead."

I let that soak in because I sensed he wanted it to.

"Why do you haunt this battlefield?" I asked him. "Why does it haunt *me*? The next time you see me, I will have an answer."

"But it may be wrong," he said.

"Yes, I know," I said, and we wallowed in laughter on the Indian mound until I rolled off.

General Nathan Bedford Forrest, wounded three times, acted out the ways other generals were shot, but usually with an odd twist. Riding ahead of his men at Shiloh, he was fired upon by hundreds of rifles. A ball hit his horse, another struck Forrest himself above his hip bone, grazed his spine, kept moving until it stopped in his left side. In another battle, a ball entered his left hip, roared around his intestinal region, and broke free of his body.

Yankee Sharpshooters shot many horses out from under him, four in a single battle. He once rode up to a Federal officer in the confusion of battle, but the officer yelled, "Turn back! I recognize you, General Forrest, and do not wish to see you killed!"

Like General Jackson, General Longstreet, and maybe General Ashby, General Forrest was shot by one of his own men, but in this case the man's identify is clearly known, and he deliberately shot Forrest, who had accused him of cowardice. Forrest, wounded, held the officer with one hand, there on the railroad station platform, and using his teeth, pulled out the blade of a jackknife and stabbed his assailant.

When someone at Appomattox asked who was the greatest soldier under his command, General Lee's answer was, "A man I have never seen, sir. His name is Forrest."

I never saw either Forrest or Lee, either one, or General Sanders, not face to face.

What was General Forrest doing during the siege of Knoxville? (Was he ever in Knoxville?) He was then commander of operations in West Tennessee.

Although now all agree, even Sherman, that Forrest was the best cavalry commander, the fame of Stonewall Jackson, General Lee, and others renders General Forrest missing—from public consciousness.

Why am I drawn to General Forrest? Were time not running out, I would track him down more closely. He had on-target ground vision, not tower, omniscient vision like General Lee or General Longstreet. But then again, maybe what he had was severely limited omniscient vision, the gift he needed.

The Tennessee River doesn't act like other rivers. From Knoxville, it dips into Alabama, then flows northward into Kentucky and empties into the Ohio. Caught between the Tennessee and Cumberland Rivers is a long, narrow strip of land. Near the Kentucky-Tennessee border, I took a look at Fort Donelson at Dover, where General Forrest refused to surrender his cavalry with the fall of the Fort to Grant. Where, they say, he slaughtered his Negro Union soldier prisoners.

I remembered that somebody once told me a story about this strange, isolated place, but I can not remember the story itself.

I wandered up the Land Between the Rivers. The tales folks tell as I wander, about the great earthquakes around here sixty years ago and of the mystery craters and caves, make me see a smoky desert with fires flaring and what they call "blooms" of iron coming out of the furnaces, carried for miles by mule-drawn wagons to riverbanks.

In Stewart County, I sit under a tree, sketching the abandoned Great Western Furnace, a single link in a vast chain of furnaces that stretches across Middle Tennessee, many, most in East Tennessee, now defunct. All the trees within sight of me are young because charcoal was the fuel for the furnaces. La Grange, Bear Spring, Mount Vernon, Cumberland, and Piney, and a few others are the only ones still in operation, and as I moved through Dickson, Montgomery, and Stewart Counties, around those names hovered the ghostly names—I like the sound—of furnaces now obscured by vines and briars: Orebank Hollow, Upper Forge Branch, Iron Hill, Blooming Grove Forge, Sailor's Rest Furnace, Washington Furnace, Lafayette's Furnace, O. K. Furnace, White Bluff on Turnbull Creek, Eclypse Furnace on Leatherwood Creek, Rough and Ready Furnace, Dover Furnace, Bellwood Furnaces, Cumberland Rolling Mills Furnace.

A fellow here told me the Great Western Furnace was built by Newell Company in 1854 of limestone from the hills around here. It is a steam, cold-blast charcoal furnace. Slaves dug brown iron-ore from shallow deposits about two miles north. Pig iron was shipped by river or hauled to rolling mills to the east. "As it turned out, there was not enough ore around here to keep the furnace going anyway, but it only lasted two years," said a man who appeared out of nowhere to guide me, "because the slaves who worked inside rebelled and killed their masters."

I crawled up inside to see what it looked like from the inside out. Folks around here tell it that the slave laborers had a foothold of less than a foot wide as they worked the burning charcoal in heat and smoke that was too intense for a human. As I sat there trying to imagine how it was, I saw the Negro soldier who set up his shebang right against the deadline post under my guard tower at Andersonville, and I imagined him, who could speak and read and write Cherokee Indian, as an intelligent creature in bond-age to the owners, working inside that pigmy pyramid. Was he the one who told me a story of this place? I disremember.

Even though I crawled up in there—the original entrance was blocked by fallen limestone—and walked around inside on the narrow ledge and looked up the flue, the stack, where the smoke had poured out, where the sun now poured down on my head, and then sat down here under this tree to draw the furnaces, I feel as if I am in Bleak House tower looking through a window down on all I see and imagine. Even if someone had only described this Great Western Furnace to me and told me its story, I am certain that what I would have imagined would not be very different from what I see now as plain as the nose on my face (which others see when I do not).

Are any events solitary, unique? Even bizarre incidents have parallels. The Shaker motto Reverend Carter once quoted to me, "Every force has its form," has been my own. I have tried to find or make or capture the form of the force that thrust me on a trajectory over the years of the war and after, and since I came back from the West. I feel the sadness of knowing that I have failed to find the form, to find a way of seeing the form of the force at work.

The more I listened and sketched, the less I tended to talk, until I became inarticulate, almost a stutterer, until I was mute, but somehow just my presence, walking or drawing, maybe the way I walk, my gestures, and, I reckon, my eyes (cross-eyed, the right looking out into the future, the left looking back into myself, into the common past) makes men gravitate toward me and orbit around me and commence to wag their tongues. Much of what they tell, they saw no more than I did. And still I do not have the same compulsion to repeat to each of them what I have heard earlier from others.

All this time that I have been drifting back over the battlefields, I real-ize more and more that it is all between the covers of books I could have read by the fire on the Mountain! While men, boys, like me, fought only in fits and starts here, there, over yonder, and everywhere, seeing no more in bright sunlight than if it were nether darkness, as if it were all one frayed strand, men with pen and ink fought the whole War.

A man showed me two drawings of Sharpshooters at Devil's Den at Gettysburg, dead in their nests. One looks a little like me and, of course, could have been me if the trajectory of my movements and those of Minié balls had intersected at the right time, in the right place, as they say. "From a Photo," it says under the drawings. My host says Mathew Brady was the photographer. I have learned to be skeptical.

I feel an affinity for these illustrators, the ones who were there and the ones in New York City who copied the photographs of battlefields before or after, but added the action photographers could never capture. Why, I wonder, do I *devour* these drawings of the War? I have only sketched, with a pencil, never charcoal, never attempted painting, as some of these artists later did. Sketching seems to verge on photography—the speed of taking a likeness, sometimes as fast as the five-minute exposure of plates to sunlight, but without the long wait to develop them in the darkroom wagon.

I look for myself now in these drawings, for some likeness to what little I remember. Sometimes I redraw the drawings made from photographs, like the one of the dead Sharpshooter in Devil's Den. Although I have already determined that the rifle in this picture is not a Sharpshooter's rifle, I get the feeling something else is wrong in this scene. I wish I could put my finger on it.

A language of the hand precedes facility with a language of the mind, from drawing to listening and writing. But as I listen more, the more facile becomes my pencil, too. (I hear a grindstone whirring, my intellect the blade, circumstance the wheel, my will turning the handle.)

I know that I experience the war most sharply when I see it through the emotions, the imaginations, the intellect of others—not just veteran soldiers, but veteran civilians, like Reverend Carter. I'm not sure what I feel and think about that.

•

Bleak House Tower

THE HOUSE WAS DESERTED. THE FRONT DOOR OPENED WITHOUT A SOUND.

"Did you come to see 'the prettiest shot of the war'?"

Even here? Yes, an amateur guide stepped out of the shadows.

There at the end of the grand entrance hall was the fresco on the wall that the artist was working on when General Longstreet commandeered the house. Had he kept working on it during the siege and the battle and after we vacated the place, and did I smell back then the paint of the wet fresco? I remembered that the blood on the wainscot in the tower looked like the drippings from a brush.

"For a silver dollar, I will tell you the whole story."

Was he the man I drew in Pulaski? No, but what difference would it have made if he had been? I gave him a silver dollar.

"Come over here." He took me by the arm and stood me in the wide doorway of a large empty room. "See that hole? Go ahead, you can stick your finger in it. They all like to stick their finger in it."

"No, this silver dollar is for letting me be by myself." I wanted to go up in the tower alone.

"But that's the hole the Yankee artillery put in the music room wall while General Longstreet and his staff walked up and down, trying to decide what to do next. The 'prettiest shot of the whole war.'

"And don't forget to go up in the tower and see the bloodstain on the wall that can't nobody wash off no matter how many times they try. Just spit on it and rub your finger over it and you'll see for yourself what I'm talking about."

He took hold of my arm. Something in his grip made me feel his grip on sanity was weak. I broke loose and walked out of the house. Maybe, I thought, I'll come back later.

No, I didn't want to go up into the tower any more. And I never have to this day.

I met a man out front of his house just below the place where General Sanders fell. I know little of other battles. This one, I know by heart. But I couldn't stop Mr. Anderson from telling it, without, I could sense, hurting his feelings.

"Across Kingston Pike from Bleak House tower just west of here, with Third Creek at his back, General Sanders deployed his seven hundred cavalrymen. That way, he blocked us on the ground from the East Tennessee and Georgia Railroad to the river. Desperately—because his greatest achievement could be only to delay us while Orlando Poe strengthened the fortifications we had begun ourselves just before the Yankees occupied Knoxville.

"The Eighth Michigan got behind rail pilings from the road to the top of the hill across the pike there, on Jacob Thomas's farm. That lone cedar tree yonder stands in the center of their line of defense. Seventy-five yards behind that tree, General Sanders commanded the line.

"But he often climbed the steep bank above the railroad track to the leafless cedar tree and directed the fire. The Yankees used the seven-shot repeating breechloading Spencer rifle that fired fifteen rounds per minute."

I said, "We could fire *our* muzzle-loading rifles only two accurate shots per minute. We talked a lot about that." If he picked up on that, I felt I might let him draw me out.

"We spent all day November 17 establishing our lines around Knoxville." Mr. Anderson used "we" in a tone I recognized as that of the citizen spectator who had not served. "Except for the high ground across from the river where we were most expected to.

"Jenkins's infantry moved east to the Tazewell Road, to discourage any retreat plans Burnside might be shaping. Might be. But probably wasn't.

"Most of our Confederate soldiers were concentrated from Middlebrook Pike, west of Third Creek, to south of the river. The cavalry moved all along the arc as far as Boyd's ferry. Our supply line was simple and easy.

"If Burnside acted as General Longstreet willed him to act, he would escape east, and in the open country, Rebel cavalry and reinforcements coming down the valley from Virginia would put him out of the war business.

"At about noon of the 17th, General Kershaw decided it was time to assault General Sanders's position. But General Kershaw couldn't get our men moving against General Sanders's troops because, from behind their fence rails, they kept us penned down.

"'Powder and shot are too scarce to waste on isolated pockets of resistance,' said Colonel Alexander, commander of our batteries. He was eager to bombard those forts that we'd started and that Orlando Poe was finishing. We had to give it up when dark came."

And I slept in the cold, damp tower, where during the early morning and that day, I gestated a chest cold.

"At Crozier's house, Burnside and Sanders talked over their situation. I learned later on, of course, about that meeting. At about 11 P.M. Burnside sent for Poe and asked how long it would take for the troops to advance the works to a defensible condition. He estimated by noon next day. Burnside asked Sanders whether he could maintain his position until noon tomorrow. Sanders said he was confident he could. "

The next day a Sharpshooter shot him.

"A man on a white horse was seen riding along our lines," said Mr. Anderson.

I have been told that a mysterious rider, on a phantom horse, appeared before numerous battles.

"They say General Sanders rode up to the front just as Confederate infantry was making a frontal assault on the hill and the railings. We were astounded that he could hold the position hour after hour against greatly unequal numbers."

Telling about what he saw first-hand only bits of, heard about soon after, then read about years later made it all as if it happened yesterday, so that "we" came naturally.

In the tower, I watched a few Yankees now and then leave their position behind the piles of fence rails, their only cover on that bare hill, and begin to fade backward in retreat. Then an officer (General Sanders I know now) would appear on the crest of the hill, half his tall frame erect above the rails, exposing himself to the terrible fire at close range until every retreating man returned in shame to his proper place in "the scheme of things," as Reverend Carter always says.

In the tower now were seven more Sharpshooters in addition to the original two, three, if you include myself.

Mr. Anderson was still telling it. "McLaws's infantry gave General Sanders trouble in keeping his promise to Burnside—he was clearly a man keeping a promise to somebody, himself, certainly to Burnside and Poe.

"Many of the casualties were the work of the ten Sharpshooters in the tower at Bleak House." It occurred to me that this gentleman was telling my own story to me and that I was listening as if I had never heard it before.

"General Sanders sent a request to Benjamin at Fort Loudon to put a few rounds into Bleak House tower.

"The gunner fired, the powder smoke cleared, and Poe and Benjamin saw through binoculars the hole *in* the tower, and six Sharpshooters running from the tower."

I was so feverish with the cold that had gone from my chest to my head that I did not know at first why six of the men were crawling on the floor and down the stairwell, two of them head-first. The only men who did not leave the tower were two wounded men, the young Virginian about my age, and me.

"The shell did not really strike the tower, but the wall downstairs beneath the tower. It went through the outer wall, travelled across the library, and lodged in the opposite wall. Longstreet was down there with Kershaw and Alexander.

"'That is the prettiest shot of the entire war,' said Captain Poe.

"About noontime, General Longstreet said to Alexander, 'The assaults of our infantry are not going to do the job. Destroy those fence rails with your howitzers.'

"General Sanders had kept his promise. But Poe asked him for two more hours, encouraged, as General Sanders was, by Benjamin's damage to the Sharpshooters' nest above Longstreet's headquarters.

"For two hours Alexander's howitzers scattered fence rails to all points in the compass and skyward, but the Federals gathered them up with astonishing speed and stacked them again.

"General Longstreet then ordered Colonel James D. Nance to lead the 3rd South Carolina Infantry in a direct charge against General Sanders, while Colonel John Kennedy led the Second Carolina on a flanking movement on Sanders's right.

"'See those two lone cedar trees,' said Nance, 'not the one at the center of their lines, but those two? About thirty yards in front of their lines? I want you to advance to that point and take the rails,' said Nance, 'then stop. Alexander will order Captain Taylor to open fire with two of his twelve-pound Napoleons and Captain Moody's Louisiana battery will shower the rear of the rails with shrapnel from twenty-four-pound howitzers.'

"When the Rebel cannon fire first began, General Sanders, his aide Major R. E. Lawder, and Colonel Wolford left the safety of the area behind the bank and walked up the steep hill to the trees. Then he and Lawder walked to the center of the line.

"'The line is beginning to break,' General Sanders said. His men were backing away from the rails and dashing down the hill behind to safety.

"Nance raised his sword and yelled in a great bull voice, 'Forward, guide left, March!'

"We rose up and rushed across the road to the foot of the hill.

"'Double quick march!' yelled Nance.

"The Second Carolina swept in from the right.

"The Third Carolina charged up the hill.

"General Sanders watched the 8th Michigan begin an enfilading fire upon our advancing men.

"The Federal officers rallied most of their men back into line behind the rails and fired into our boys with renewed fury.

"The 3rd South Carolina held their fire until they reached two cedar trees about thirty yards in front of the rails. There they halted, dropped to the ground, and commenced firing. That must have looked odd to the Sharpshooters in the tower, and sure enough our boys had misunderstood their orders. They had stopped at the two cedar trees instead of at the fence rails where the lone cedar tree stood."

"The young Sharpshooter from Virginia blurred my vision," I told Mr. Anderson, "and I saw a narrow stream of blood appear between the Virginian's knees where he knelt and move toward where I sat leaning against the blind West wall.

"So I thought, well, I'll see what's going on out there, and I crawled across the floor to the narrow window beside the Virginian and looked out at the bare hillside that rose across the Kingston road. Then I sighted through the sights of my telescopic lens. And I saw a man, an officer, riding a white horse, *charging* back and forth in front of the Yankees that was firing at us. He's going back and forth like he's daring them to kill him. Shoot! Shoot! I'm here! Shoot! See if you can *do* it! Riding back and forth. And I thought, Nobody, on their side or our side is crazy enough to be doing what I'm watching, it's fever, it's fever got me, you know. Why, hell, I can just shoot at that feller and it won't even hurt him. That's kinda nice, shoot somebody that you can see plain as day, I know it's a fever, you shoot at him, won't even hurt him, I just shoot him, won't bother him, you know. I pulled the trigger, and I just turned away, I didn't even see if I *got* him. I thought, 'Well, maybe my stray bullet will accidentally kill one of those Yankees behind the fence rails.'"

I realized I knew "My Story" by heart. Mr. Anderson looked amazed to hear *me* talking a blue streak. I had told him what I could never tell Reverend Carter, unless I wanted to turn him against me. But Mr. Anderson was so absorbed in telling *his* own version of the skirmish, he didn't show whatever it was he thought about *my* story.

"Captain Stephen Winthrop, an Englishman, who was once captain of her Britannic Majesty's 24th Infantry, was serving with Alexander's artillery battery near Bleak House. He had watched Nance's infantry charge the rail piles and stop by mistake at the two small cedar trees, caught in the enfilading fire, unable to retreat. Recalling the charge of the Light Brigade, I always like to think, Winthrop leapt onto his horse and rode swiftly across Kingston Pike. The only horseman in the skirmish, he rode through our troops who lay on the ground firing, and up to the fence rail piles where the enemy, a hundred strong, were firing at him as he charged."

I plunged ahead on my own. "I crawled back to the West wall and leaned back against the cold brick, and looked into the wide open eyes of one of the wounded men who seemed to have been watching my odd behavior.

"'Did you get him?' the man asked me.

"I smiled, closing my eyes, thinking, 'He's in so much pain, he doesn't even know the Virginian is dead.'"

"I see. I see. Well," said Mr. Anderson, "a Minié ball struck Winthrop's collar bone, broke his scabbard, took off the tip of his sword, and he collapsed upon his horse's neck.

"General Sanders and Lawder had stood under the lone cedar tree at the center of the Federal line, awed by the sight of the brave cavalry officer.

"Bullets passing over their heads from the rifles of the Confederate brigade that Winthrop's lone charge had rallied, they turned and started down the hill out of range.

"'What a gallant fellow he was,' General Sanders testified to Lawder, who heard a bullet hit General Sanders. 'I'm hit! I'm no further use, go, leave me here.'

"Lawder caught Sanders in his arms, but he weighted two hundred pounds. A few men helped him carry General Sanders about four hundred yards to the rear, then to my own house, I regret having to say. History puts that burden on me forever."

Mr. Anderson invited me into his house, saying I needed some hot coffee.

Surrounded by books, he wanted to tell me more of it. Mr. Anderson reminded me a little of Reverend Carter. I was eager to hear him tell what it all meant.

"To continue, Sanders bled profusely.

"'We surrender!' they heard some of their men yell.

"The firing ceased.

"Lawder's men turned an old ladder into a stretcher for General Sanders, way he told it. They crossed Third Creek, started into town with him.

"When the Federals heard that General Sanders had been hit, they started firing again.

"The sudden reversals stunned Nance, who ordered his men forward again.

"The South Carolinians made it to the top of the hill, jumped over the piles of fence rails, and looked upon thirty dead Federal soldiers. They stripped them, and took their haversacks.

"Nance's men took charge of the hill and surrendered to fatigue.

"In his report Nance, who along with Kershaw's brigade had taken the force of the assaults in the second day of the battle of Gettysburg, said, 'It is but truth to state that this was the most desperate encounter in which my command was ever engaged, and as it was perhaps one of the most brilliant charges of the war, I cannot speak too highly of the conduct of my comrades.'

"Nance had no way of knowing that in the memory of Captain B. F. Thompson, 112th Illinois, many years later, *he* had been killed that day. 'Colonel Nance rode up to within thirty yards of our lines and demanded we surrender. Major Dow of the 8th Michigan politely told him to go to hell, and ordered Corporal Williams of Company A to shoot him, but others fired at him and he fell dead in our front.'"

And unlike me, Thompson wasn't even delirious with fever that day.

"But maybe the sight of Captain Winthrop's British dash bedazzled Thompson," said Mr. Anderson, "for it was Winthrop who demanded he surrender and it was Winthrop himself who got shot" (accidentally by me, perhaps) "though he didn't die. Colonel Nance got nary a scratch."

"Winthrop's reckless dash," I said, "was an exaggeration of all those many other reckless actions in which generals were wounded or killed."

"Lieutenant Colonel Alfred O'Brien of Louisiana, brother of Parson Brownlow's wife," said Mr. Anderson, riding over my attempt to find some shape to all that force, "said the Union soldiers were new troops that didn't know enough to run, and that all his men had to do was go up on the hill and haul them in.

"But our men couldn't holler the green Yankees out from behind the fence, so they forced us to turn back several times. In that clash, 119 Federals were killed or wounded, 75 captured, with 140 Southern casualties. Our Colonel Gist (brother of the General Gist killed later at Franklin), the 15th South Carolina commander, was killed."

"Do you know, I wonder," I asked, "whether he is kin to the Gist who was Sequoyah's father, as some records state? Some say Guess, not Gist."

"I wouldn't know that."

The story Mr. Anderson told me of the shooting of General Sanders contradicts the story I wrote for the Elizabethton newspaper editor but did not publish, the story the man I was sketching in Pulaski, Tennessee told, and that Mr. Anderson told me was the story Knoxville historians Rule,

Humes, and Temple tell—of General Sanders riding a white horse out front of his men on Kingston Road, and of a Sharpshooter in the tower of Bleak House shooting him.

"I know because I have read the Official Report now," Mr. Anderson told me, "and Alexander's and Poe's versions, too, and the one I have just told now is the factual truth.

"The details of the wounding of General Sanders are, as the saying goes in such cases, 'Shrouded in mystery and controversy.' Jake Warren, who later became sheriff of Monroe County, takes credit for shooting General Sanders off his horse. Hiram M. Vineyard tells the story of how he picked a general on a white horse as his target and shot him off his horse.

"The way the Rebel attack forces were deployed, any number of men could have shot General Sanders deliberately or accidentally, but none shot him off a horse, white, gray, or black, because according to the man who stood beside him on the hill, Major R. E. Lawder, General Sanders's aide, the story I have just told you is the true version of what happened. Lawder visited his brother-in-law Captain W. P. Chamberlain in Knoxville, and in talking with folks, he declared that General Sanders was wounded just as he had finished watching, with Lawder, Captain Winthrop's stirring charge.

"Even after others have agreed with Lawder, the story you hear still in the streets everywhere, and that you find in several so-called histories, is the legend of General Sanders on the white horse riding out in front of his men on the Kingston Road."

I thanked Mr. Anderson for the coffee and the facts and went my way.

I, too, like the legend, especially if I don't have to carry the burden of actually shooting him in that way myself. But I miss the mystery. When the man I was sketching in front of the hotel in Pulaski, on my way home from the West, told the legend and took credit for the shooting from Bleak House tower, I didn't remember even being in the tower, and his story stirred up in me that sense of having missed the war, until several years later I was inspired by that feeling to tell my story, as much of it as I could remember. In the act of telling what pitiful bit I could, I remembered being in the tower myself, and my fever, and seeing the general on the white horse and firing at him as a magnificent fever-image.

That horseman, I know now, could only have been Winthrop, but attacking the hillside north of the road, *not* down on the Kingston Road riding west, recklessly ahead of his men, exposing himself as Jackson, Longstreet, Johnson, Stuart, and A. P. Hill had, but even more recklessly. When, or if, I fired, I missed Winthrop or only wounded him, for he was indeed wounded, but not killed.

My own action is stretched so thinly over a range of probabilities, possibilities, and unlikelihoods that I confront the question, Was I the right man in the right place at the right time, or the wrong man in the wrong place at the wrong time, or both; simultaneously, somehow, or neither? I can't even be certain I was ever in that tower. The man I sketched in Pulaski could have planted that seed, for my brain was like plowed ground. I can't be certain I had a fever and saw an image or a real horseman. I could have been quite well and lucid and taken deliberate aim at the officer, Sanders, or officers, Sanders and Lawder, standing on the hillside, exposed, as they watched Winthrop's charge on the white horse.

Or the young Virginia Sharpshooter who was killed—By whom? I would like to know. Why have I never asked that question until now? Has that been an accidental or a deliberate omission? Was I jealous of the attention Longstreet gave him?—*he* could have shot General Sanders as he stood on that hill.

What interests me almost as much as the answer to the question is the way the legend-making impulse in people selects actual ingredients and immerses them in imagined ones. It is a fact that Winthrop on his white horse charged out in front of his men. It is a fact that General Sanders was shot in the same place, on Kingston Pike west of Knoxville. Those two facts strike the legend-making vision and spark its imagination, which places General Sanders on the white horse down on Kingston Pike riding West alone, out front of his men. The Sharpshooter in the tower is then imagined as the agent of the general's wound.

What really happened is imperfectly perceived, complex, and messy. The legend is simple and neat. And beautiful to contemplate. It has shone brightly in my telescopic sights for decades.

I had a feeling that to walk Fort Sanders would put a keel on the whole maze of my search, a gyroscopic steadying of the whirl.

Of all the battlefields of first and second rank in fame, I can think of very few that are, for *other* reasons, important places today. The naming of forts and batteries after fallen soldiers, or renaming them if they were first named by the enemy, is strange. As Poe's work went on and on, at the old works and at the erection of new ones, the names of the recently killed were given to those forts and batteries, until most had Union names, replacing some Confederate names from the time they held the town only three months before the siege. That's very strange to me, and rather awesome and silly and moving, a way of monumentalizing the dead while animating the spirits of the living for that twenty minutes that is the time span of so many great moments in so many major battles, for most of the time is devoted to preparation and survival tactics.

I met on the site the Virgil of Fort Sanders battlefield who is about twelve years old and whose name is Lucius. He lives two miles west but he seems compelled to be over here telling it to whoever will walk the field with him and listen. There are rolling hills all around here and a graveyard over yonder under some fir trees. A sad, lonely, sick-sounding boy, my Virgil says he knows more about this place than anybody because his daddy died here.

He carries a Minié ball and a casing with a hollow in the back of it, and as he tells the story, he is constantly tapping the Minié ball into the hollow part of the casing, saying often, "As I was telling you yesterday," but I was elsewhere yesterday. He doesn't really know *all* the details, but feels as if the things that must be told are what he knows. Old mud on his shoes from tramping over the field every day. Talks of sawing off the limbs of the wounded, or as *he* says it, "winded," as in winding a watch. No enthusiasm in his voice for his self-assigned task, but as if forced to the front of the room by his teacher, condemned forever to recite, "Stacks of limbs like wood," in the tone of "2 x 2 = 4."

I wanted to tell him the epic of the battle, but many before me had already told him, and I have told you in "My Story," and I have only a few thoughts to add.

Somebody ought to write someday a mythic Civil War battle, one that combines all the major elements of all the battles. All the bridges, for instance, leading up to and those on the battlefields, including the plank across the ditch at Fort Sanders. I see all the decisive battles, the Sunken Roads, at Shiloh, Gettysburg, and Antietam, stone walls, cornfields, orchards, bloody ponds, hornet's nest, bloody angles, and the underground explosions, all repeated down there below the tower at Fort Sanders, without the famous names monumentalizing them.

General Longstreet seemed to me then an omniscient being—though

Reverend Carter had to give me the word for it—while looking as real as leather and brass. Strange now to realize that from up in my tower then, I could have seen as *deep* the ditch he saw from horseback as shallow. He never climbed up into the tower itself.

When the men reached the ditch, they found out it was not four feet deep, what they'd been told, it was as much as eleven feet deep, as men have told it ever since.

Actual events that had become the historical past were for General Longstreet fantasy possibilities as he surveyed the hard realities spread out before him.

I remembered the former Confederate arsenal, still containing some live ammunition, blowing up, and the many buildings of the railroad machine shops, and many houses, burning against the cold night sky, lighting up all Knoxville. Many voices spoke of the fire that night, and again in the years after at different times, and mine now joins them, I *in*spire now the witnesses of that night, for breath is fire, spirit is fire, and to inspire is to 'breathe life into.' I draw on all those fire phrases in the military lexicon: "field of fire," "all-searching fire," "fire power" in my field of vision.

Time affects memory the way acoustic shadows affect witnesses to battles. The phenomenon of the acoustic shadow that made the battle of Perryville silent was experienced and later reported several places elsewhere—and probably other places not reported. Air masses can render the omniscience of generals null and void. Is it thus that drowning men, calling to shore, are often not heard?

That there is some correspondence between strange external weather effects and odd effects in the weather of the mind I do not doubt. Do I think these Mountains are thinking because *I* am thinking? Or am I thinking because the Mountains are thinking?

I was there, but not there. Even now, I must turn to not even an officer who was there, but to a civilian who has taken over only this one small battle, who has become the authority on whom I rely. I have heard so many of these details from so many people now that I shall never in my life be able to separate what *I* actually saw from what other people say *they* actually saw. The Sharpshooter's necessary vantage points enable him to see more than infantrymen, but his missions are also singled-minded. Sometimes after battles, even the commanders had to look at the maps (often drawn *after* the ceasefire) to see what had happened.

I have tower vision, and now a kind omniscience. The melancholy necessity to know the truth results in the melancholy of knowing that the truth is never complete enough.

I wanted to know more about General Sanders after he was carried from the battle and before the fort was renamed in his honor. I headed east on Cumberland Avenue for Gay Street, the street where I had asked for directions to the War when I was a boy, searching now not for the truth, but for somebody's own passionate version of the truth.

On Gay Street at Cumberland Avenue, I gazed upon the Lamar House Hotel, which had been converted into a hospital during the War. To this place General Sanders was carried, mortally wounded, and placed in the bridal suite.

When I asked at the hotel what had happened there, nobody could tell much—the manager offered to show me the bridal suite, vacant at the moment, but I declined to see it. A man loafing in the lobby told me to ask Reverend Humes. "Old Unionist. Writing a book about the Loyal Mountaineers of East Tennessee."

"The Humes family built this hotel originally as a residence in 1816, you know."

I went around behind the hotel to the Reverend Humes's present residence adjacent to St. John's Church.

We sat on his porch while he told me the story of the death of General Sanders.

"'At about half past two he fell,' his friend Captain Poe has written, 'mortally wounded, and the screen which he had so stubbornly interposed between the enemy and our hard-working troops was quickly rolled aside.'"

No, he wasn't telling it, Reverend Humes sounded as if he was speaking from the book he was writing, from memory, quoting what somebody else, Poe, had written.

"Porter Alexander, learning of the wounding of Sanders, said to General Longstreet, 'We had been intimate at West Point and had met in San Francisco in 1861, as I was about to resign to go into the Confederacy.'

"At 3 o'clock, as General Sanders was being transported up Kingston Road, which becomes Cumberland Avenue at Third Creek, into Knoxville toward Gay Street, Rebels moved into positions closer to the Yankee lines and the siege of Knoxville began.

"Dr. J. C. Hatchitt, who was an old friend from Kentucky, found that a bullet had entered General Sanders's left side and torn his spleen.

"'How serious is it?'" asked General Sanders, whose mind was clear and calm at that stage.

"'The wound is mortal, Willie.'

"General Sanders's comrades in arms kept the death-watch around his bed all through the night in the bridal suite of the Lamar House. For three days he lay, surrounded by ministers, surgeons, friends, his mind unclouded.

"'Soldiers, I am not afraid to die.' He wanted to ease the anguish of the men who sat and stood around the room. 'I have done my duty and served my country as well as I could.'

He heard the sounds of a besieged city through the windows, distant bands, pickets firing at each other occasionally, starving horses and mules screaming.

"On the morning of the 19th, Doctor Hatchitt told General Sanders, 'I must tell you that you have but a few hours to live.'

"At 10 A.M., the Reverend Mr. Hyder, post chaplain of the Methodist Episcopal Church, baptized the general at his request. He was thirty years old.

"'I am glad I was not shot in the back,' he said, and as he slipped into delirium, he repeated that over and over."

Had he always feared he *would* be? Why? His last words made me wonder.

As if right before my eyes, I can see that the written word has become sacred, replacing the events themselves.

"'Then the minister in prayer commended the believing soul to God, General Burnside and his staff, kneeling around the bed. When the prayer was ended, General Sanders took General Burnside by the hand'—Major Barrage, 36th Massachusetts Regiment, wrote this in *The Atlantic Monthly* in 1866—'Tears dropped down the bronzed cheeks of the chief as he listened to the last words which followed. The sacrament of the Lord's Supper was now about to be administered, but suddenly the strength of the dying soldier failed, and like a child he gently fell asleep.'

"A soldier unknown to history broke the silence by saying, 'Let us pray.' He held up the Episcopal Book of Common Prayer, bowed his head, and lifted up his trembling voice, 'Oh Father of mercies and god of all comfort, our only help in time of need, we fly to Thee for succor.'

"Major Lawder testifies that they all wept like children."

As, I was told, General Longstreet had wept for the young Sharpshooter from Virginia.

"When they got back to Crozier House on Gay Street, Burnside told Poe and other officers, 'Longstreet's troops have advanced to the ridge where General Sanders was shot. They have moved within rifle range of the defenses on the northwest, from the river above to the river below, in an arc. Knoxville is besieged. There is need of constant vigilance and alertness upon this long line of defenses. Those in command cannot, therefore, prudently leave their posts of duty in daylight. We cannot assemble them for the funeral of their slain comrade. It must be conducted in secret and in darkness. No music, no death march, no rifle salute over his grave. That hurts me deeply.'

I imagined Reverend Doctor Thomas William Humes, president of East Tennessee University, writing *Loyal Mountaineers of Tennessee,* memorializing my own grandfather, father, and brothers among the rest.

"'In the afternoon, a resident minister of the Gospel,'" said Reverend Humes, speaking of himself in the third person, 'was requested by General Burnside to attend after nightfall the funeral of the officer, whose wound unto death had signalized the beginning of the siege and thrown a dark shadow upon the spirits of his companions. They gathered together at their commander's headquarters, and among them was the Chief Engineer of the Department, Captain Poe, who was a personal friend of the deceased—his only class-mate at the siege—actually Porter Alexander, another classmate, was on the other side—'who spoke of him as a "most gallant, chivalric soldier and noble gentleman."

"'As the party of mourners passed down Gay Street to the hotel where the body lay, General Burnside spoke of the extraordinary personal daring of the departed man. With sad emphasis, he said, 'I told Sanders not to expose himself, but he *would* do it.'

"'Upon reaching the hotel, the company's number was increased by waiting friends, and after religious offices a procession was formed upon the silent street. There was no plumed hearse, drawn by well-fed horses, but kindly hands of brother-soldiers to bear the dead, at the end of "The path of glory that leads but to the grave."

"'A sort of—a sort of weird solemnity invested the darkened scene. Its features were in such strong contrast with those which might be expected in the fitness of things it would wear. No funeral strains of martial music floated on the . . . the. . . .'

"Now, I want you to hear this part exactly as it is written in my book." He went inside and returned to his chair on the front porch toting his manuscript, already well-thumbed. "'No funeral strains of martial music floated on the air. It seemed as if War, disrobed of its pomp and pageantry, had taken its departure, and its absence was supplied by heaven-born Peace, clothed in plain and simple attire, disdaining through profound grief all trappings of woe.'"

The trappings of rhetoric threatened to bury General Sanders before he reached the grave. I don't mean to mock. I warm to the idea of Reverend Humes, Judge Temple, Editor Rule, Mayor Heiskell, members of a tribe, whose leader is Doctor J. G. M. Ramsey, of local historians, but such flourishes do not fit all occasions and I felt the need, on that occasion, of the natural voice of a witness, but for what I was hearing, the occasion called for a translator or interpreter.

"'An observer might fancy that the army, which with dauntless courage refused to surrender to men in superior force, had now surrendered to God, and that its chieftains, having yielded up their swords, were marching along the way into captivity.

"'But yet, not all is peaceful. For hark: there comes the sound of booming cannon.'"

General Sanders's classmate, now enemy, Porter Alexander on the other side?

"'And every little while it again peals forth upon the hushed air. From the presence of these night obsequies, War is gone, but he lingers near and bids defiance to the encroacher of his domain. Little heed, though, do the mourners give to his hoarse notes. And the heavens appear to sympathize in the grief, for their face is covered with mist as with a veil, and hanging low in the western sky, a young moon sheds her dimmed luster on the scene, and from above all, the loving eye of One looked down, without whose notice, although He rules the army of heaven, not a sparrow falls to the ground.

"'At the head of the procession went the Commander-in-Chief and the minister.'"

Humes himself, of course.

"Well, read the book when it's done," said Reverend Humes, who had taken many years to haul out all those words, words seldom heard coming from the mouths of men.

I politely urged him to finish the story man-to-man.

"'By their side walked the Medical Director of the army, bearing a lighted lantern in his hand.

"'Said the clergyman, 'I am reminded of Wolfe's line on "The Burial of Sir John Moore."'

Moore, Reverend Humes told me, was killed at the moment of victory over the French in Spain in 1809. Have you ever noticed that some ministers are always reminded of everybody but the person they are about to bury?

"'General Burnside quickly replied, striking his hand on his thigh, 'I have thought of those lines twenty times to-day.'

"'That lantern did duty at the grave, as the body was committed, "earth to earth, ashes to ashes, dust to dust," in hope of the resurrection of the dead.'"

Some say and write no shot was fired, and Humes told of none, but he said Poe wrote that the silence shook him, he nodded to other officers, and they raised their pistols in the air and fired a salute.

Maybe *I*, in my tower, heard that pistol salute, and the music someone else said was played, but I can't swear to it. I can only listen to somebody tell what he read about it.

"'When all was over,'" Humes went on, "the general said to the minister a thoughtful word concerning the event, inevitable, awaiting all men; and then every one went his way, some to watch and some to sleep; but probably few of the company could forget the burial of General Sanders in the likeness of its circumstances to the 'Burial of Sir John Moore.'

NOT A DRUM WAS HEARD NOR A FUNERAL NOTE
AS HIS CORPSE TO THE RAMPARTS WE HURRIED,

Not a soldier discharged his farewell shot
O'er the grave where our hero we buried.
We buried him darkly at dead of night,
The sod with our bayonets turning,
By the struggling moonbeams' misty light,
And the lantern dimly burning.

Slowly and sadly we laid him down
From the field of his fame, fresh and gory,
We carved not a line, we raised not a stone
But we left him alone in his glory.

"As Poe and Burnside left the grave site, Poe said, 'With your permission, General, I will change the Rebel name of Fort Loudon to Fort Sanders.'"

Humes then got on with the business of the siege, word for word.

I share Burnside's and Humes's liking for the parallels between the poem (I copy from Humes's book) and General Sanders's funeral. I suspect, though, that Reverend Humes made his account fit the poem more than the poem the actual events. All three versions—Hume's and the Poet's and Poe's—move me, but only a little.

The unmarked grave line—"We carved not a line, we raised not a stone"—proved more prophetic than Reverend Humes knew at the time. He kept it dark where "at the grave" *was.*

"Most people," I said to Reverend Humes, "say it was in the cemetery of Second Presbyterian Church in the west block of Prince and Union across from the Market House."

Many people suggest that since Humes was the minister of St. John's, General Sanders was buried in the yard of St. John's, not Second Presbyterian. Clashing war sentiments had split Humes's church, so he had closed it, but Burnside asked him to re-open it, and only Unionists were admitted. Second Presbyterian was born of a split with First Presbyterian in 1818. The building went up in 1820 and was replaced in 1860. Second Presbyterian was a Rebel church, so the Yankees turned it into a hospital, as the Rebels had turned First Presbyterian into a hospital.

I walked over to Market Street to take a look at where General Sanders's grave *might* be.

A fellow said, "They have moved General Sanders's grave."

I imagine General Sanders's grave at both cemeteries and can't decide.

Some time later, nobody can tell me for certain, General Sanders's body was reinterred in the National Cemetery at Chattanooga. Many other soldiers have lain in more than one grave. His family, divided in their loyalties, seem to have neglected his grave, for there is only a government marker, giving his name and his volunteer rank. His sisters married wealthy men. But his mother applied out of great need for a pension and was denied, because, some conjecture, General Sanders's three Rebel brothers were officers in the cavalry of three Mississippi regiments. I was, in some ways, like General Sanders, with my family on one side and me sharpshooting for the other side. How, I wondered, would my family have treated *my* grave had I died a Rebel soldier? Another tale removes his body to a third grave somewhere in Minnesota. I've pondered all this a long time and can fix it in neither logic nor imagination.

You could tell the history of the war, couldn't you, from cemeteries, ending perhaps at the great stone memorial pyramid in Richmond's Hollywood Cemetery?

And from inside strategic church structures, a body could tell a history of the Civil War. All the churches in Knoxville—as most towns and cities—were converted into hospitals. In the photographs, I see Dunkers Church at Antietam, the most memorable focus of the slaughter in the cornfield, whiter than any other church, like a whitewashed tombstone, waiting to take in the bloated dead who lay on their backs on the field around it. At Fredericksburg, the church steeple from which I fired upon the damaged railroad bridge over the Rappahanock. I still hear the boards creak underfoot.

I had steeple, belfry vision there. What if I had had steeple vision from the start, from the Mountain to Andersonville Prison?

I walked across the Gay Street Bridge at Knoxville, that the Yankee military built. In the second block, I stood before the building that served as the prison where they took me just before I became a Rebel soldier. It was now a schoolhouse.

I walked past Parson Brownlow's house on East Cumberland, but did not see him. They say he usually feels pretty low.

I walked out of Knoxville and through Strawberry Plains, where Reverend Carter's Raiders forgot matches to burn the bridge there, through

Bull's Gap, where I fought with General Longstreet, through Jonesboro, Parson Brownlow's home town, through Greeneville, Andrew Johnson's town, where General Morgan was shot in the garden of a lady friend, through Lick Creek, where my brother Tim and other bridge burners were hanged from an oak close to the tracks, so Rebels on passing trains could strike them with their canes for burning that bridge.

Troops had crossed and burned the bridge behind them several times throughout the War and now it bore the burden of its history.

"It's a sorry sight," I said to an old man fishing off the bridge.

"Well," the man said, "you know what General Sorrel said, don't you? 'No man should curse the bridge by which he safely crosses over.'"

"I feel that in my very bones, sir," I said. "You know, you could tell the history of the whole war by sticking just to the bridges."

"Yeah," he said, spitting over the wobbly guard rail, "and you could tell the story of the whole war from the cab of a locomotive or without even taking your foot off the railroad track."

Reverend William Blount Carter, Architect of the Master Plan to Burn the Bridges

As I got closer to my cabin on the Mountain, I knew that everything would become clearer.

In January, 1877, I was home again.

I went down to visit Reverend Carter and told him everything about my trip.

He showed me "my recent acquisition": Alexander Gardner's *Photographic Sketch Book of the Civil War*. "It cost me a pretty penny. I've been eager for your return so I could show you this one photograph in particular. See here, the dead Rebel Sharpshooter in Devil's Den at Gettysburg?"

"I've seen several different drawings from this photograph."

"Do you see anything wrong with this photograph?" Before I could answer, Reverend Carter plunged ahead. "First, let me tell you that I have seen a photograph of Alfred Waud, the battlefield artist. As Waud sat on one of the boulders in Gettysburg, sketching for *Harper's Weekly*, Alexander Gardner's assistant, Timothy O'Sullivan, photographed him. Waud looked as dashing as any cavalry hero.

"Now, look here at this view of rocks," Reverend Carter said. "Notice the white pad lying on the rock on the right. I imagine it belonged to Waud, who left it there. Now here is the question, Did O'Sullivan and Gardner, looking for corpses to shoot, find Waud sketching at Devil's Den?"

"Or did Waud," I asked, my eagerness startling Reverend Carter, "looking for a vantage point from which to sketch from memory, but now from the Confederate Sharpshooter's point of view, find O'Sullivan and Gardner there?"

"Or did they meet elsewhere, and did Waud, who had witnessed the battle, lead the two photographers to Devil's Den?"

"And what is it Waud is sketching in O'Sullivan's photograph?" I wondered, aloud.

"Perhaps it is the place where General Reynolds fell, the sketch of his I have seen most often."

"I have put it together this way, sir."

"Let me see," said Reverend Carter, "if *I* can imagine how you have figured this out. O'Sullivan turns from taking a picture of Waud to help Gardner find and choose a scene to capture. They find the Sharpshooter's nook—empty. But they imagine a Sharpshooter lying dead there."

"They *see* a photograph of him."

"O'Sullivan and Gardner carry a body forty feet—probably a young infantryman—in a blanket—" Reverend Carter persisted, "—because where he had actually fallen, he did not look interesting."

"Up between two boulders," I put in, "high as a tall man, was a stone wall, built in the heat of battle, but nobody lay dead there. So they stretched the corpse out there, turned him into a Sharpshooter, into a photograph, there where I had made a wall the night before." I had let it slip out, my identity as a Rebel soldier was there in the room for Reverend Carter to look at, but he seemed not to have caught my blunder.

"It is O'Sullivan who actually exposes the plate." Reverend Carter, flushed, combative, plunged on. "Light becomes an accomplice to their fakery, their fiction, this icon now of the War. Gardner gave him credit in a catalog, but took credit himself when he sold portfolios of his prints in 1866."

"Then *Harper's,* under the woodcuts based on the photograph, gave credit to Mathew Brady."

"Excellent, Willis," said Reverend Carter, his voice weak with some new attitude that his loud applause made me suspect as envy and resentment. "You know, O'Sullivan was among the many war photographers who followed the transcontinental railroad and army survey parties. The Indians called him shadow-catcher."

"I imagine him after the war, wandering the West, just after I left there. While I wandered aimlessly, he wandered to satisfy intentions."

"I see," said Reverend Carter, "I see."

"At Devil's Den, where many sight-lines had criss-crossed three days before," I persisted, "the sightlines of artists and photographers converged." I saw in Reverend Carter's eyes the recognition that his sightlines and mine were among them. But now I was on my own, seeing, learning, teaching. "I missed my own death in Devil's Den, I missed 'The Harvest of Death,' but Timothy O'Sullivan and Alexander Gardner faked my death in one of the most famous photographs of the war, famous up to that year mostly in the drawing rendition, however. THE HOME OF A REBEL SHARPSHOOTER, GETTYSBURG. Then the wrong photographers took or got credit for it. I realize that what you and I see is after all a product of Gardner's and O'Sullivan's combined—"

The expression in Reverend Carter's eyes, of one bereft of an insight he had felt unique to himself and had waited eagerly for my return to teach me, abruptly made me stop. And then the startled look of recognition came to his eyes—the knowledge that I had confessed who I was. I was a veteran of the Confederate army whose bridges he and his men, in league with my kin, had burned.

I backed away from him, turned and departed his parlor, knowing I would never be welcome again.

Climbing the Mountain paths, I finished my thought, with the intention of fixing it in writing. I realized that what I see in that photograph is after all a product of Gardner's and O'Sullivan's combined imagination, with Waud as possible encouraging witness or even third participant.

Many sightlines converged in Devil's Den, as mine do now.

I missed my own death in Devil's Den, but O'Sullivan and Gardner missed what those who saw the famous photograph, and the drawings various artists made from it, saw: a young Rebel Sharpshooter dead in Devil's Den at Gettysburg. O'Sullivan, who took the photograph, and Gardner, who took the credit, could never, can never see what I saw and imagined.

"If the Ash-Heap Begins to Glow Again . . ."

Nineteen years later, I was ready to write Going Home.
I am almost certain now that I did not shoot General William Price
Sanders. I hear many voices talking about General Sanders. The man who
said he shot General Sanders, as I sketched him at Pulaski. Many others.
Telling fragments of a story that remains scattered.

As I leave off these violent meditations forever, in the winter of 1913, I
am sixty-five years old. I live alone. I can no longer see well to hunt. A
young Carr—he is named after my brother Tim—comes up to look in on
me, bring me food, other supplies. He uses the cabin for shelter when he's
hunting.

I have re-read these fragments. To my "descendants," whoever you turn
out to be: Read me aloud. In those fragments, I am speaking to you—
whoever you are who finds them, hidden in parts of the cabin. Is that *you*,
Tim?

I want to imagine simultaneously and daily all the dead in my family and all the people I knew who are now dead, and all I have only heard about.

Even as I read, I *heard* voices; what I read returns in memory as voices. What is written was first spoken in the mind's auditorium, then read aloud to oneself or to friends, or aloud by those who now read the words.

So many accounts of each event, mostly conflicting, have gone through so many different kinds of processes.

Lives other than our own. . . . As someone other—I must become *others,* male and female, Rebel and Yankee. Having been a soldier, I have willingly imagined myself a civilian ever since. Because I thought I probably killed him, I willfully imagined myself General Sanders—I even wrote scenes as if I were a real writer writing General Sanders's story, and burned them.

Because I missed all those battles, I tried to imagine the battle of Fort Sanders as the *one* battle. I who did not burn, burn. I who did not see, see. I who could not read, read. I who perhaps killed, perhaps live. In *being* what I am not, I *become* what I am.

While connecting one thing with another, especially opposites, I may connect with what is essential to my own emotional, imaginative, and intellectual well-being. In striving to experience through others fully what *I* missed, I reached the realm of the impersonal. Feeling, imagining, thinking neither as General Sanders nor as myself. Because of General Sanders, whether I killed him or not, and through him, I have achieved over the years, for a while, what Reverend Carter experienced—omniscience, of a sort, and felt the simultaneity of events, actual and imagined. Now, I could probably imagine everything in detail if I set about it, and had life left, time.

Sequoyah combined the needs of the day and history. Like Sequoyah, I tried in my various writings to begin again.

Over the years, I have read as much as I could find about Sequoyah. But he, too, seems missing. I want to set his story down, but I do not feel just right about it.

That autumn of 1875 when I started telling my story to my editor friend, in a recurrent dream, a voice repeated, "If the ash heap begins to glow again. . . ."

Come forth, Greatgrandfather Carr, through whose voice all other voices filter, whose tone and timbre test all others, inhale, exhale, inspire, expire, body's blood the threshing floor of utterance, and before these testify—that was my mood when I started telling it.

Having told it, I have re-experienced it, and I am born again. That is what I tell myself.

I *know* now most of the available *essential* facts. But that is not enough to let me rest. Most of what I know now about the war that I fought and killed in, I got from eyewitnesses later—and from books. I hate my ignorance as if it were a disease. I want to get cured. Facts are like medicine. I want to *know.* Or my ignorance is like a human enemy I must slowly conquer, a hostile neighbor. Ignorance is bliss, though—until what you don't know kills you.

I make lists, and count, and compare, and contrast, and parallel, *to see.* Dates anchor.

Everything is in a name.

Names of places tell where, and suggest what and how and why. But newspaper headlines are snares.

Even though I am obsessed with fact-finding, I can not swear authenticity for what I have written or may yet write. My imagination leads a life of its own. I did not knowingly, of course, traffic in errors. That a fact proves later to be an error does not alter its earlier status in *experience* as a fact. So what I felt in response to the "fact" was actual, not an illusion. My feelings about the new error status of what I took at first to be a fact are on a much lower scale of emotional or intellectual value.

For every misperception or delusion about "What happened" there is *a* truth. If this man or that man did not do such and such, someone else, somewhere else, at another time, *did* do it.

I studied it all over. Then what I tried to do was to string some of it out so I can now look at it. Once I get it all in own sights, I might write me a proper book, too, to pass it on. But now, words, pictures are all I have to pass on, no children.

You, whoever you prove to be, must collaborate with me in a conspiracy against the tyranny of mere facts. Each man is duty-bound to conjure, call forth, breathe life into, imagine. I see Parson Brownlow coming. Look. Coming—distance, like a thunderclap, vanishes, and he's standing on a bridge.

Parson Brownlow was often called a demagogue, which many of his Mountain friends misunderstood as Demi-god, and *that* they only vaguely understood. When you read the *Whig,* his *voice,* like a conflagration, was what a body heard. Cold type became live coals, and you smelled the brimstone. His words were bullets. The voice itself was already injured from the early decades of preaching, debating, orating, but I hear it still raving as he composed his editorials.

He carried over from Methodist circuit riding and the camp meeting into journalism a sense of danger and risk, the force of passionate professing. His mind, voice, print—were a single torrent. In speech, he repeated what he had printed; in print, what he had spoken. Did he *think* at all, meditatively? Or only on paper, as a circuit preacher thinks only on a wobbly plank thrown across two stumps?

From the homes around Knoxville and East Tennessee and far, far beyond, a copy of the Declaration of Independence or even the Bible might be missing, but the Parson's editorials were often nailed with a stiff YES or NO to the wall by the fireplace. Men, and women, turned the cold type back into hot, uttering breath. Inciting Unionists to insurrection or taunting Secessionists with thumping irony, his editorials—and the *Whig* was all editorials and advertisements, information and news being buried in the commentary itself—were banked fires that readers stirred alive, roaring or raging with laughter.

For many years, I liked to imagine I was conceived after one of the Parson's camp meetings and delivered after the next one.

I wish I could trace back the trajectory of blood into what became me, July 25, 1848, the year the Mexican-American War ended. But I know only my father's line, and only back to the man at "the place of fire." I do not know my father's mother's name.

From childhood, I don't remember hearing the other last names on my mother's side. Her folks never came up to see us, so I never heard their names called, and when I visit my mother and her new family, I do not ask her. So I am only a Willis and a Carr. The other trajectories of blood are missing.

I sometimes feel I am one of Lucifer's angels, slow to land, not on a lake of fire, but on a Mountaintop. For I missed the fire, too, only a witness, not a firestarter, even though those five bridges have been burning in my life since that night my daddy, my brothers, and my grandpa set one of them afire.

Leaving my Greatgrandfather behind, I set out, like the other men in my family, _to fight in a war,_ knowing nothing really about war, about this War. Both sides said, "They are trying to take our land, our homes, rape and kill our women and children." I had no definite feelings about either side. In the Parson's book, I find, "The word was in mine heart as a burning fire shut up in my bones." Unlike John Wesley—and Parson Brownlow and Reverend Carter, the planner of the bridge burning—I had no fire in the heart, in the head. I heard that as a child Wesley was saved from a fire in his house. Years later, his heart grew warm, and that moved him to convert. Wesley's fire, the Parson's fire, Carter's fires scorched others. Maybe me, finally. But back then, I just wanted to go to war and do it. I plunged. I still feel as if I am on a furlough from death. Born into Death, I am not, as people like to say of themselves, living my life, afraid of Death. We are always dying our death daily.

When I went in, I was thirteen, when I was a Sharpshooter in the tower, I was fifteen, when I went West after the surrender, I was seventeen. The question comes at me: Why do I feel and remember so little? I know now that I was there and I was not there. Immaturity is a frustratingly partial answer. And my memory is clouded by the two-year drunk in the West. Neither physically nor mentally mature, I was, nevertheless, "there."

Though not at the beginning. I followed some of them when the five bands of raiders rode down out of the Mountains to burn the nine railroad bridges up the Great Valley of East Tennessee from Chattanooga to Bristol. But I set no bridge afire.

When I left this Mountain, I did not know that before He got to me, God had done his work on General William Price Sanders, and all the others.

It is hard to hit moving targets. Just when I get a man in my sights, he moves and sets General Sanders in motion down Kingston Pike toward the Tower, the legend on horseback, not the man on foot on the hill.

I did not know that He started something unique in the brain of Sequoyah, the Cherokee who was the only man in history to invent a whole syllabary.

I did not know that he created Alexander Gardner who is known as the photographer of the dead Rebel Sharpshooter.

I did not know that before He created Knoxville, He created the Carter Settlement where I was born in obscurity and raised in ignorance, and that I would never _see,_ until I climbed into the tower in "Bleak House" and *saw* a general on a white horse riding alone, too far in advance of his men. I did not know any of that.

No, I never did. But now I know. And knowing, I have felt compelled to tell it, beginning with the burning of the bridges on the Grand Trunk line in the Great Valley of East Tennessee.

Looking out over the slopes of South Mountain so many years, it has got to where now, I no longer feel I am in Bleak House tower, no, I am always in the guard tower, I see all of them clearly and, suddenly, my father in a Yankee prison, Cahaba probably, even Andersonville possibly, who survived and was going home with four hundred other East Tennesseans on *The Sultana,* and I see him, and his countrymen, and all those at Andersonville, together, drown now below me.

And Grandfather Mississippi Death has claimed most *Sultana* survivors.

Somebody happened to say "Andersonville" the other day and I was in Andersonville before I knew it. Twilight. Feeling sad.

I have this dream often lately: Andersonville, not as it was the day I arrived, but as I *almost* saw it again in my battlefield travels twelve years later, and only read about it, saw the few drawings and, later, photographs of it, and heard men tell about it.

I drink from Providence Spring that the great storm started up out of the ground, to deliver men from filthy Sweetwater Creek that still, men say, bisects the camp site. That guide who is always there in such places is eager to tell me, pointing everything out, eagerly.

Standing in the guard tower, I see thousands of captured Yankees, starving, dying of disease. Looking for them, not finding them, but expecting suddenly to *see* one of my own kin, brother Jack or Bob, or my father. My knees go weak and I wake up.

I dream that dream often. But in recent days in broad daylight, I begin to imagine Andersonville, and remember.

I am near about ready for the Messenger.

Cherokee's Story

Now! Last evening out hunting on South Mountain, skylarking, looping my leg over a sycamore sapling the afternoon lightning storm laid across my path, I said out loud, "Over the deadline!" almost as a joke—on the other side, Cherokee lay dead.

I looked down one day from my sentry box at Andersonville Prison and this big black buck was bracing his back against one of the deadline posts, reading an old yellowed newspaper for all the world to wonder at. I thought he was set on tormenting me.

"You making fun of me?"

"Making fun? I'm reading my newspaper." Without seeming to look up from the paper, he snatched a fly out of the swarm around his head.

"You pretending to read that thing?"

"Now! I will tell you!" he said, "I have known how to read since I was five or six."

"You lie."

"No lie." As he snatched another fly, I imagined mastering that feat myself.

"Let's hear it."

He ripped a piece of it off, smooth as bear grease, but I didn't catch a word of it clear.

"You're making it up as you go along."

"No, I ain't making it up."

He stood up and offered to pitch that paper up to me to prove it.

Sure he was bluffing, I said, "Making fun of white boys who can't read any better than you can might get you shot." He laughed and danced around, not knowing how close to perdition he was.

I called a halt to that, but he couldn't help himself, couldn't stop it, and even got me to laughing, and when he stopped, I believed him.

Then it scalded my cheeks to know I was an illiterate who was looking at a nigger that could read—a Yankee nigger at that. No, that wasn't so bad, because what did you expect of Yankees? I had almost forgotten by then that, except for my Rebel mother, I had come from an East Tennessee Unionist family myself.

❧ ❧ ❧

From my sentry box looking West, I see the crack of dawn on the face of an old man in a sentry box opposite me. I watch the compound turn slowly and then all of a sudden into an open grave swarming with maggots. Like a sudden agitation of a stagnant pool—the men on the hillsides. And the simple hell of daily life begins. The mosquitoes prick like needles.

A loud groan, the gates swing open on massive iron hinges, rusty from decades of other use, but bolted to fresh-smelling lumber. In comes the deadwagon to gather the 130 or so who died in the night. Out of these 25,000 survivors, I will watch about 130 more die today. Two months ago in March, they tell me, it was only 30 a day.

Behind the deadwagon, a new prisoner in a dusty but fresh uniform stops in his tracks on "Broadway," the main street. Gaping at the sight of two hillsides thick with starving, sick, dying, and dead, he faints.

Behind the new prisoner, almost naked, stands one of the corpses that went out stacked on the deadwagon yesterday morning. He had to lie all day in the deadhouse, then he rose up in the night and ran—into a circle of bloodhounds, like all the others who pretend to be dead.

My gaze meets a boy's gaze. Many guards are under fifteen, and the one across the grounds—I can see the crown of his cap moving inside his sentry box and now and then his nose and eyes as he raises himself up on tiptoes, looking for a chance to shoot. The rumor promises thirty days furlough if we kill a Yankee.

Yesterday, a boy shot himself accidentally, or maybe to get relieved from guard duty.

A man crossing Sweetwater Creek on a single plank bridge takes hold of the deadline, too dizzy to balance, and a shot rings out from one of the fifty sentry boxes around the wall.

In this stream, I wash my clothes and soldiers water horses and mules, and buckets, tubs, kettles are washed there, and I watch it pass under the hospital, then it passes under the wall and crosses the compound. Men are walking over to it, using it as a sink, pissing and shitting into it.

Men crowd around the sutler as he opens his shop inside the gates. Sour beer is the brew.

A naked man drops a piece of bread and accidentally kicks it under the deadline post, reaches for it, and joins his comrades in another world.

A company near extinction by daily dying rides their Jew comrade about the camp on a rail for being absent at roll call. Distribution of their food was delayed because of the missing Jew.

From the tower, I watch Collins, ironically called Mosby after the leader of the famous Rebel Raiders, lead his Raiders among the other prisoners, who part like sluggish waves to let the villains through.

As I look over the compound, over the wall, at my tent among the tents, where I wish I could still be sleeping, the sight of tents inside the wall makes me feel the difference among we men who guard and these men who languish.

Men are fighting over a dead man's shirt, almost killing each other until it comes apart rotten and they stagger backwards with a sleeve, a cuff, the tail in their hands.

But one hides a cap behind his back. If he can get out on wood-gathering detail, he can trade that cap for onions, potatoes, beans, or something, and sell them inside at sky-high prices.

Two men are roasting what looks like a grayback, a rat.

A man buys a button of soap and staggers down to Sweetwater Creek that bisects the compound in the narrow valley between the two hillsides.

The smell rises to my nostrils of dysentery, the sink, "invalid's retreat," the dead in state under the brush shelter outside, weird foods the men have found to concoct and cook, the swamp itself, horse shit, logs and lumber and canvas baking in the sun, and smoke from the fires outside and the desperate little fires inside, and of trains, and over it all, like mockery, bread baking.

And when I eat what they send up to me, all those smells come out in the taste, I gag, and eat, and gag, and it is *gone* by the third or so bite. And what I smell and taste up here seems lifted on sounds, of bugles, horses neighing, hounds tracking escapees and animals, the homesounds of whip-poorwills or bob-whites, mosquitoes, guns firing, sometimes as if many miles away, though only up the hillside somewhere, metal clinking, or if I am on watch in the night, the hooting of owls, the zip-by of bats.

I watch the Raiders try to recruit other prisoners to join them and share their spoils.

I look down at the man who writes in his diary in the first light of each morning, as if the terrors of the night were part of each day. "I am the only one writing a diary," he says aloud, to himself. I do not tell him that up here I can see many others writing in diaries all over the compound.

The prisoners use most of the paper with print on it to wipe the splatters of diarrhea.

Before my eyes now at once, I see all the stages of sickness: sores, fevers, lassitude, dropsy, scurvy. Many have gangrene. A man who looked healthy yesterday rolls out the gates on the deadwagon this morning.

On the men, I see a chamber of horrors exhibit in blistering daylight of instruments for torture and punishment—barbed iron collars, ball and chain for those who go outside to work, stocks, thumbscrews, shackles, men hanging by their thumbs. None of the instruments are new-looking. Used before, on slaves. Maybe that newspaper-reading buck wore them as a slave before the War and some time in here before I came.

Raiders attack the prisoner who fainted and beat him without mercy, steal his blanket, and try to sell it to the guards.

"Can I reach over to kill that snake?" I hear a man call up to a sentry nearby.

"You can," says the old man in the sentry box.

As the prisoner reaches over the deadline to club it, a shot rings out, he falls, and the snake glides off into tomorrow. Another guard hadn't heard permission given and so had shot him.

I watch sailors and soldiers fighting on the higher of the two hills, north, and down below where I stand watch, marines and regular soldiers are fighting again.

But other men read and some write as the sun gets hotter.

They bring in more black prisoners.

Captain Wirz rides through the gates on a white horse. Dismounted, he walks among the men, a pistol in hand, the men shouting, "Hang him!"

"Now! We call him 'Death on a Pale Horse,'" says the buck Negro below me.

Whispering, just to show I know something myself, I say, "They always tell of a rider on a white horse in every battle."

"We also call him 'The Flying Dutchman.'"

Wirz has to pass the cemetery, I think, when he goes home.

Citizens, men, women, and children come to stare at the prisoners and turn up their noses and laugh.

For the naked men, some wearing only a greasy cap and broken shoes, baked black as slaves by the sun, I feel embarrassed.

Artillery is being moved.

"Rumors of Sherman nearby," whispers the Negro. "Wirz has a lot to worry him. Sheridan's and Sherman's raids and rumors of their movements caused a great fear last winter before I came."

Wirz places a cannon on a hill and tells these thousands who have survived, "If Sheridan or Sherman come within one hundred miles of Andersonville, I will open up on all of you!"

"He did the same thing a few months ago," says the Negro.

A man climbs a ladder up into my sentry box and with the help of several men pulls a camera up after him and sticks his head under a black cloth. I try to see what he, or the camera, sees.

When he leaves, I am moved to draw the scene, but as if I am higher in a tower by myself, looking West. I remember that the West wall in the tower at Bleak House in Knoxville was blind, bricked. Remembering drawing those wounded and dead men on the wall, I draw a map of my life: South Holston Mountain, Bleak House tower, this sentry box in Andersonville Prison, so I can *see* where on earth I am.

The men seem to be creating a police force to deal with the Raiders. Negroes and Indians and whites band together for protection from the Raiders.

Men come to the Negro below and cup their hands and whisper into his ear and he listens and thinks and then slowly nods.

The very smell of the new wood makes me feel a sense of the slaves putting up these buildings—hospital, church, cook house, officer's stockade in case there's a mass break-out, and the double walls of this pen—in a big hurry to take the pressure off the prisons in Richmond. I imagine all the trees in solitude that once stood here, now cut down, shoved, lashed, nailed, bolted together, leaving not a single, solitary tree inside the walls. "They shall have no shade."

One man staggers vomiting against the rail. A boy guard shoots the prisoner and yells in derision, "Man on parole!"

I watch the Negro pick lice from his clothes.

Wood is precious. Men scavenge for it, hoping the Raiders won't take it from them.

I watch an Indian give his white officer a smuggled sweet potato. I can hear him below me tell his dying friend, "We get out all right."

I'm not about to help anybody escape. I don't even feel like talking to any of them. That black buck keeps drifting over to my tower, too close to the deadline—only eighteen feet between rail and wall. I know he's trying to take up with me. Why, I can't say. But it's really me that started it with that question, "You making fun of me?"

"What's your name?" I whisper down to him, afraid to be seen talking—or even listening—to a prisoner.

He gives me an Indian name I can't pronounce so I don't call him anything yet.

"My father gave me a name, white boy!" He says it again, but again I can't say it.

I have to talk secretly and he has to pretend not to look at me when he talks. But it's as if he can throw his voice, so he seems right behind my left shoulder, my best ear.

"How do you throw your voice like that?"

"Now! I am a shapeshifter. My master's father could throw his life into a treetop and show his body to a hundred men firing at him. But one day, one of his enemy knew he could do it, and told his friends to shoot into the tree, and my master's father standing on the ground fell dead, his chest full of arrows and bullets."

Some slaves are sent in to inspect the wells—"Love's Delight," "Jacob's Well," "Heart's Ease"—for evidence of tunneling.

"Slaves built this place," whispers the black buck, "and were still at it even as the first trainload of prisoners came in."

Too bad he came in after those other bucks finished their work. He could have disguised himself as one of them and slipped away into the swamps. Since they don't ever find any tunnels and escapes soon prove that they existed, they might take a liking to this big buck yet.

"Now!" he said, starting to talk. I asked him why he says, "Now!" like that and he says, "That is how Cherokee Indians start their letters when they write to each other."

"You lie. You ain't no Cherokee Indian."

"Now! My granddaddy's white master in Georgia sold my granddaddy when he was a boy to an Indian living at Chota, the capitol of the Cherokee Nation. That's twenty or so miles southwest of Knoxville, Tennessee. That was before the Great Removal, and my daddy was born in Tellico Plains, near Fort Loudon. My mother and father were taken on the steamboat *Knoxville* from the Overhill Territory to Nashville, and then on the long trek over the Wilderness Road, the Trail of Tears. My mother died giving birth to me. So when this war commenced, I had no love for the federal government.

"Now! My father had been a translator of my master's and the white man's speech, and I became one myself, at home and in this War."

"Did you forget your grandfather's African way of talking, or did you ever know it?"

He doesn't seem to want to answer and goes on talking. "My Cherokee master was good to his slaves, especially to my father.

"Now! My master violated a new law that was made in the new territory by teaching me to read and write. Cherokee writing, letters and newspapers, and we even had books in Cherokee, the Bible, too."

He was the first person, prisoner or prisonkeepers, to talk to me. All the other prisoners treated me as if they thought I wanted to shoot them to show I was trustworthy. They respected my ability and feared me. He did, too, but was talking to me—we were talking to each other—me asking questions.

♣ ♣ ♣

Captain Wirz announces he is withholding food until the Raiders are captured by the other prisoners and put on trial.

Beatings and murders every day and night down there.

I draw a prisoner in a newer uniform sitting beside a man in a ragged one, lying down, and in the contrast, I feel the process of decay.

An Indian has grooved a piece of wood to make a washboard and hung out a sign, DO WASHING. Men come to beg him to join in fighting the Raiders. He says, "No time to fight now. Must do wash."

Many have hair a foot long. That Indian cuts the hair of one of his friends, maybe dreaming of scalping enemies in days gone by.

Our flags are at half mast for some of *our* great men, to oppose the prisoners' Fourth of July celebration for the Union.

Some of the Raiders are being arrested this morning. A few almost got lynched.

Five men killed in battle between the Raiders and the new prisoner police force. A hundred died today from disease. One man wandered in a daze across the deadline. They were all buried in the same trench in the cemetery. The guard who died today was buried in the Rebel cemetery. A guard dies every few days.

I see a friend sell the corpse of his friend for fifty cents. You get to go out with the body, so men will pay to pose in your place as the tentmate or closest friend, so they can barter outside the walls with the guards or try to escape.

When I am on duty at night, I hear men crying and shivering.

"Post number five!" I call out, and forty-nine other guards sing out the same. "One o'clock and all's well!" Somewhere else in the world, I reckon.

They are arresting more of the Raiders this morning. There goes the leader, Collins, or Mosby, as they call him.

Somebody told Wirz that six thousand men were plotting to escape. The officers persuade him it is a joke to make him prance around.

Men are still digging tunnels down inside the wells.

"Now! You think war is bad?" the Cherokee Negro whispers up at me, eating bug soup and pretending not to look my way. "This War is nothing to what is going on back home between the two factions of Cherokee. There's the Treaty Party, who are most like the white man in their ways

and who own slaves such as me and my folks. Then there's the National
Party, who want to keep up their ancient traditions and rites."

I wish I could listen to some of them talk, as the Cherokee Negro is
talking to me, about *their* War.

"The Yankee soldiers say they have to go in there every few years and
slaughter a great many of us to keep us from destroying each other altogether.

"I am afraid for my family in that holocaust.

"I want to trade this little reservation you are guarding for the one I left
back home in the Territory."

The Indian grubs for roots to boil.

Others are gathering roots to burn.

The new prisoner who fainted when he saw his new home is now plumb
crazy.

A band plays "The Girl I Left Behind Me" for a large crowd from
Macon, picnicking on grounds a mile off in sight of many of the men.

Tennesseans come in. I look for grandpa and daddy and Jack and Bob.

"My folks is Union," I tell Cherokee, my name for the black buck.

"Then why are you guarding Union men?"

"You say you are a Cherokee Confederate, but what I am guarding is a
Union Soldier in a Rebel prison." I think he is lying though.

A sane man calmly folds his arms and without breaking stride loops his
leg over the rail into oblivion.

"Now! I grew up in times of constant Civil War," says Cherokee, as if
to the buzzards that never stop circling. "Leaders of one faction assassinated
treaty-makers with the white men when they returned from Washington.

"And when the War for Southern Independence broke out, the Confederacy looked to Cherokees still in the East and one faction in the West
for support. Some wanted to be neutral. But most go either with the North
or the South.

"When my master's son Stephen set out for Memphis to join the Rebel
army, his father gave him a slave to take with him, just as white plantation owners do. But he called me his brother.

"The Cherokees had slaves before the white man came and first enslaved some of *them*. But their own slaves were always enemies captured
in battle, considered not human for not being kin. They didn't make
slaves of Africans until the rigid rules of kinship among the Cherokees

withered a little. They enslaved Negroes only because, from their first contact with Negroes, they saw them in servitude, and never saw them in any other condition.

"Cherokees called themselves 'The Real People,' so anybody who was not their kin were worse than animals. Since Indians did not work, they never thought of making their slaves work. But when they started doing as the white man does, very hard work had to be done. Rich white Southerners did not work, so rich Indians bought Negro slaves from the white man to do their work for them.

"But being a Cherokee slave was not as bad as being the slave of most white men. I found that out when I saw more of the world in the War with the son of my Indian master. When Master Stephen was captured, the Yankees forced me into their army."

"Forced? You didn't want to fight and kill Rebels?"

"No, I hoped they would turn me loose, so I could go back to my people."

"What people?"

"The Real People, the people of the Cherokee Nation in the West, where my wife and babies and other kin live, where my old master lives."

"But don't you want to be free?"

"Yes, free to go home. Listen, one time the Cherokee captured twenty white boys, little boys, and ten years later, white soldiers rescued them, and they cried all the way back to the white settlements, till they almost dried up like beanpods in October. A man starts from where he is.

"Now! Listen. My brother was no translator. He refused to learn Cherokee, he ran away to Tennessee, to the Land Between the Rivers and was captured and forced to walk around a pit of molten steel on a ledge only one foot wide, inside a furnace no bigger around than a tee-pee, for eighteen hours a day for the whole two years that the Great Western Furnace lasted."

Between the wall and the deadline, Sweetwater Creek flows cleaner water, so two men reach for it and a guard, an old man, shoots them.

"Slaves were forced inside that furnace, the overseers keeping tight watch, themselves choking on the charcoal and ore smoke, the smelting process, a smell they'll never get out of their nostrils, feeling the white-hot heat on their own skins, but not as intense—not until they were thrust into the foundry and fire of the rebellion.

"I sometimes dream of that isolated place, the workers, slaves, and over-seers, enduring, surviving there, the owners safely somewhere else in the cities in the North."

A great cloudburst interrupted, stirred up a dormant spring, a short distance north of Sweetwater Creek. Pure water appeared so miraculously that the men shout its name all at once—Providence Spring!

The storm washed out part of the wall and the men stole the logs to burn for fuel. Slaves are bringing in fresh logs and closing the gap.

"How did it end, Cherokee?" I whispered.

"Don't call me by a name that is not my own!"

"How did it end?"

"Now! My brother led a rebellion. The slaves killed their masters and other white men killed all of *them,* except my brother, who escaped. He lives in Liberia now, father of a large family—in freedom. A man starts from where he is, even if two men start from the same slave house."

Cherokee let that sink in.

New rumors of exchange. President Davis wanted to parole all prison-ers in exchange for some of ours, but Grant shot back, No! he had plenty of men himself, and since we were short, he didn't want to fill our ranks with Rebels from his Northern prisons.

Preachers don't come. Oh, one Catholic Priest comes, regularly, but no other faith. Some men have taken to preaching themselves, beside Provi-dence Spring.

A man was drawing something with a crude pen dipped in ink he made from rust. I asked to see it, but he wouldn't show it.

One of the boy guards shot at one man but killed the crazy man by mistake.

The Indian tells his sick officer again, "We get out all right."

⚜ ⚜ ⚜

Slaves bring new lumber in so the prisoners can build a gallows to hang the six leaders of the Raiders. Let the names be given: William Collins, alias "Mosby," after Mosby of the Raiders, John Sarsfield, Charles Curtiss, Pat Delaney, A. Munn, W. R. Rickson.

Mail comes very seldom, but it comes today. The prisoners are excited but only a few get letters.

Cherokee usually is off by himself, partly, I suppose, because he thinks of himself as a Confederate like his master, but I see him flicking maggots out of a Yankee prisoner's wound.

I watch a doctor come in with his dog, called "Parson," because he hates Parson Brownlow who is famous all over the North now for his lectures up there on the persecution of Unionists in East Tennessee. The dog wanders into Cherokee's tent and never comes out. Now the doctor is outside the double walls calling, "Here, Parson! Come to me! Now!"

"I need it to get my strength to go home," Cherokee tells me.

That makes me start watching Cherokee more carefully.

Standing down there, just back of the deadline, he cranked up again. "Now! I'll bet you didn't know that Indians are serving in the War with Confederates. They raided East Tennessee under an agent named Thomas, from the Qualla reservation in North Carolina."

"The Rebels hunted troublesome Unionists such as my family," I told him, "with dogs and Indians. I know *that*."

This morning, much of the gallows lumber is gone, carried off in the night for shelter and fires.

The prisoners have a strong police force, with headquarters, now.

Most of the men are unable to walk. They lie around in every conceivable position, some new to the human race.

More men are naked now and look like Negroes, they are so black.

"Now! I will tell you the story of Sik-wa-yi or Se-quo-yah, called the American Cadmus because he was the only man in the recorded history of the world who invented an alphabet or syllabary from scratch. And he was also called the Modern Moses because, with that syllabary, he delivered his tribes from bondage to ignorance and to the deceptions of the white man who was powerful because he used 'talking leaves.'"

"What are 'talking leaves'?"

"Listen! and you will know. Se-quo-yah was the son of an Indian woman whose name is forgotten and a white trader named George Gist or Guess. He grew up in the Cherokee village of Tuskegee near Fort Loudon on the Tennessee River, five miles from Chota, their sacred capitol. In that place, twenty-five years before, the Cherokees slaughtered their captives, the first white men and women to live in that territory. Se-quo-yah was a fine craftsman in silver work and a natural mechanic, but he had never been to a school and could not speak, read, or write English, just like some white boys I could name."

"But I never did tell you my name."

As Cherokee tells me all this, with slow gravity, I take it in word by word, the way you pick up objects and feel them to know them.

"Even though a childhood affliction crippled him for life, Se-quo-yah was a soldier in the war of 1812 against the Creeks, and fought at the battle of the Horseshoe. Sitting around the camp fires with the white cavalrymen, listening to them read aloud to each other from white leaves that came to them from far places, he discovered that *on* these leaves, many days earlier, many miles away, the family members of these men *spoke* to them.

"He was so amazed, he became obsessed with the desire for a written language for his own people, to help unite the scattered tribes, to compete with their enemies the Creeks, and to protect themselves from the tricks of white men.

"So for twelve years, Sequoyah labored to invent ways of showing the sounds of the Cherokee language in print, taking some letters of the English alphabet as models.

"In only a few hours, he was able to teach this language to his five-year-old daughter.

"But his people, who had ridiculed him all during those twelve years that he worked on it, did not accept this new language right away.

"The language was not taught in schools but from one Indian to another, using bark and the walls of houses for slates.

"By this time, he had moved with many of his people to the unknown country on the Arkansas River.

"One of the first things that was done with the new language was a translation of the New Testament into Cherokee. Then they started a newspaper, *The Cherokee Phoenix,* the first Indian newspaper in history, to which they added later the motto 'An Indian's Advocate,' out of Georgia."

He wraps a page of the *Cherokee Advocate* (its new name since 1848, the year I was born) around a stick of new timber—from left-over pieces of the Raiders' scaffolding—tosses it up to me, and the alphabet looks even stranger than my Greatgrandfather's copies of Parson Brownlow's *Whigs* were to me before I went to burn the bridges and that road ended up here in the guard tower.

"In 1821, the limping Cadmus returned to the Cherokee Nation in Tennessee and brought news of their people in the West in the new printed language."

The court convenes outside the walls. The Raiders are being tried by their own men. The trial and the hanging interrupt Cherokee's story.

One hundred more Negro prisoners come in. One had been a prison guard, I hear some say, who shot Rebel prisoners.

"In Washington, Sequoyah was given a special medal. A famous painter did a portrait of him.

"Now! Sequoyah lived ten years in the West, farming, keeping a diary. Then the Cherokees of the great forced migration started coming in. And though many had died and many came in sick and weak, the new nation began in division: the traditionalists who had always opposed imitation of the white man's ways now opposed the powerful new group of rich planters who owned slaves. Dealing with white men was always difficult because the Cherokee had been divided amongst themselves ever since their first contact with the white man.

"Witnessing the conflict among his people that he had hoped his syllabary would remove, Sequoyah had another dream. A band of Cherokee had set out years before from Arkansas in search of a kind of El Dorado in the Southwest. With his eldest son Tessee and a small party of Cherokee horsemen, he set out in the summer of 1843" (five years before I was born) "to find that wandering band."

Cherokee is detailed to go search for wood outside. Groups of three or four are sent out for firewood, sometimes try to escape, or do. Three men out of every hundred are allowed to go out after wood under strong guard. I am worried that Cherokee might escape, might not return to finish the story. When the gates squealed open, I was glad to see him come in, laden with wood.

"But an old lingering ailment, or perhaps dysentery, put him in an unmarked grave, location now unknown. His clay pipe, his journal, his medal, some of his silverwork with his famous trademark were buried with him. But not his fame as the limping warrior, the peacemaker, the forger of a new language."

Cherokee moves his shebang up to the deadline. On his knees, risking his life, he ties his shebang blanket to the deadline rail, like several others all around the walls.

"Tell it again, Cherokee."

"You know my name. Why do you keep calling me Cherokee?"

He tells it over again, several times, the whole story, and I beg to hear it.
Retelling the story of Sequoyah to myself helps pass the time when
Cherokee isn't telling it to me again.

At first it made me mad. I thought, well, hell's bells, if a damned Indian can bypass learning to speak, read, and write English by making up
a whole new reading language, himself, even if it did take him twelve years
to figure one out, is there any excuse for an illiterate white man, even if he
is still just a boy, to stumble around unable to read the language he speaks?

So I crack my head against the "talking leaves"—a copy of *Gray's
Anatomy* that one of the prisoners loaned me. But I just can't, by myself,
get past the drawings of organs and bones. I was ashamed to ask one of
the guards to teach me. And *Paradise Lost* and *Pilgrim's Progress,* that
Greatgrandfather had and that so many of these Yankees are reading now,
and I can't do any better with a new one called *Les Miserables.* Not by
myself, not with him laughing up at me.

"I'll teach you Cherokee!" he offers, to tease me.

To take the sting out of the teasing, I say, "You better, Cherokee,"
wishing I could remember and pronounce his Indian name, "or I'll put a
red frown between your black eyes!"

That tickled him, and he tossed *The Cherokee Advocate* up to me and
started lesson number one in the hot dust, reaching over the deadline,
almost getting his arm shot off by an eleven-year-old warrior in the tower
just north of mine. I set the boy straight with a little South Holston Mountain name-calling and tell Cherokee to keep at it.

Slaves come in, take the gallows apart, and I watch some of the prisoners help them so they can steal more of the lumber.

The man who writes in his diary says, "I have only a few leaves left in
my diary, but my pencil is less than a nub now." Talking leaves.

I drop to him one of my drawing pencils.

Much singing. Groups concentrate on their singing as hard as others
work on tunneling.

One man goes around shuffling, like a deck of greasy cards, a handful
of photographs of dead men's wives.

Well, Cherokee and I got serious.

Learning to read and write Cherokee language was fun but hard.

We had time, so we used it.

After a few weeks, which proved I was dumber than Sequoyah's five-year-old-daughter who did it much faster, I was reading and writing Cherokee and speaking it with him.

The Indian makes a new washboard from the hanging tree.

The man with the diary spends most of his time scrounging writing paper now.

The Indian carries his officer friend to Sweetwater Creek to wash him all over.

The two hills on each side of the creek made me see Knoxville, where there are hills on each side of the Tennessee River.

"I can't get used to talking to a black slave of the Cherokee Indians," I said. "It's like I'm dreaming."

"Well, you've seen plenty of black faces before, haven't you?"

"No. I never saw a face like yours till I went to fight. None down around Elizabethton that I ever saw and sure none up on South Holston Mountain. When I first went to Knoxville, I came and left by night, so the first black face I ever saw was a soldier in the Union army behind the sights of a rifle. I was petrified with fear, I thought his face was burned by the sun and wind. Like all the prisoners around you now are. Then I thought, no, looks like his musket blew up in his face, powder burns.

"A man next to me cursed him, and I thought he was only calling him names. 'No, that there is a nigger, sure as the world. Kill him.'

"'My first nigger,' I said, and killed him.

"Where?"

"I disremember. *My* first nigger. Not a one of us ever owned a slave, and I wasn't the only child who had to go to war to see a slave for the first time. The life I was risking, and that *he* was about to blow out if he could, was to defend my right to own and work, maybe sell or trade, that man behind the rail fence, aiming at me. At the time, I felt no sense of that, only wonder, awe, even glee at the sight of 'my first nigger.'

"Negroes have been shadowy to me in all this War. At Petersburg, Burnside selected his Negro division to make the first assault upon the crater, but Meade persuaded Grant that if the assault failed, they would be accused of allowing the slaughter of Negroes because they were only Negroes. So a much less well-trained white division went in, a fatal half hour after the explosion, and were slaughtered. The Negro division followed, but with far less loss."

"Many die of irony."

One prisoner tries to sell me a piece of the gallows on which the Raiders were hanged. I think of my brother hanging with the other bridge burners beside the railroad track, even though I wasn't certain, at that time, Tim was one of them.

The Indian says to his officer, as he says every day, I'm sure, "We get out all right."

Now I hope Cherokee—that was his name only when I thought of him, because I had stopped calling him Cherokee—will go out on wood detail and escape.

❧ ❧ ❧

"It was *The Cherokee Advocate* that almost got me shot for a spy when they first captured me," said Cherokee, "because they thought it was something in code, until an officer recognized it for what it was."

I see the graves of the raiders, set apart from and facing away from the graves of the other men.

I see the man with the diary has written two large books full. And he has another now, having bought it from a new man coming in.

A rumor has started just to torment Wirz that a giant balloon is being secretly sewn, in which men will rise above the stockade walls. He orders men to search for it. They have the look of men who feel foolish.

They hear us talking Cherokee and catch me reading it from his hands, and they get suspicious all over again.

Captain Wirz tells me, "I might have to use *one* bullet on both of you to save ammunition."

But nothing came of *that*.

All these years, it was Cherokee who was missing. I've always thought I missed the war, but it never crossed my mind that I missed Cherokee.

Now! I have written him down. He is not missing.

Cherokee never asked me to help him escape, but not until now, years later, after he's taught me to read and write Cherokee and he's made the dash over the deadline and after Reverend Carter's taught me to read and write English, do I ask myself the question that must have been hovering over me all through the decades since, "Why did I, who was raised on a Mountain and never saw a slave until I drifted into the Confederate army, shoot the slave who taught me how to read and write, even if it was only

Sequoyah's Cherokee syllabary?" Did I wonder then, "Why did he do that? Knowing I'd have to shoot him?" Did I guess he convinced himself I wouldn't shoot the man who taught me to read and write? Sure as the world, even though he was a slave and I was a white boy, I wouldn't shoot him, not even as a simple reaction? It's taken forty-eight years for the memory and the question to come to the surface, and it's possible I could live fifteen more.

Now! I am ready for the Messenger.

AUTHOR'S NOTE: IN HIS STRUGGLES TO GET HIS ROLE IN THE WAR IN HIS sights, on target, Willis Carr himself makes use, in unusual ways, of many oral and written sources; for instance, he stitches together material from the works of Knoxville historians of his time, Parson Brownlow, Thomas William Humes, Judge Oliver Temple, editor William Rule, and Doctor J. G. M. Ramsey. Willis's immersion in history and my own are the same. Although I grew up hearing the legend of General Sanders's death and was an usher in the Bijou in the Lamarr Building, where he died, Betsey Creekmore's *Knoxville* put it in focus; and Digby Gordon Seymour's *Divided Loyalties* provided me with a collation of details about the siege of Knoxville and the battle of Fort Sanders from numerous sources. For details on all aspects of Willis Carr's story, I consulted over a thousand books, too many to list here.

BATON ROUGE, LOUISIANA,
JANUARY 4, 1996

Sharpshooter was designed by Todd Duren and typeset by Angela Stanton on Macintosh computers using PageMaker software. The text is set in Adobe Garamond, a revival of the classic font mistakenly attributed for centuries to Claude Garamond, a celebrated sixteenth-century French typographer. The design was in fact the work of Jean Jannon in 1615, re-interpreting Garamond's earlier work. The display font is Engine, an extremely condensed serif design reminiscent of the exaggerated wood type used for early American advertising posters. The paper used in this book is designed for an effective life of at least three hundred years.